Dark Visions

by

Jonas Saul

PUBLISHED BY:

Imagine Press Inc.
eBook ISBN: 978-0-9869376-4-4
Paperback ISBN: 978-1-927404-79-9
Hardcover ISBN: 978-1-998047-17-8
Dark Visions
Copyright © 2010 by Jonas Saul

The Sarah Roberts Series

Dark Visions (One)
The Warning (Two)
The Crypt (Three)
The Hostage (Four)
The Victim (Five)
The Enigma (Six)
The Vigilante (Seven)
The Rogue (Eight)
Killing Sarah (Nine)
The Antagonist (Ten)
The Redeemed (Eleven)
The Haunted (Twelve)
The Unlucky (Thirteen)
The Abandoned (Fourteen)
The Cartel (Fifteen)
Losing Sarah (Sixteen)
The Pact (Seventeen)
The Terror (Eighteen)
The Chase (Nineteen)
The Betrayal (Twenty)
Sarah's Return (Twenty-One)
The Hunt (Twenty-Two)
The Delivery (Twenty-Three)
The Trap (Twenty-Four)
The Ultimatum (Twenty-Five)
The Depraved (Twenty-Six)
The Condemned (Twenty-Seven)
Payback (Twenty-Eight)
The Unknown (Twenty-Nine)
Wrath (Thirty)
The Damned (Thirty-One)
The Game (Thirty-Two)
The Decoy (Thirty-Three)
The Disappearance (Thirty-Four)
The Whole Truth (Thirty-Five)
Alex (Thirty-Six)
Parkman (Thirty-Seven)
Darwin (Thirty-Eight)

Aaron (Thirty-Nine)
Remains To Be Seen (Forty)

The Jake Wood Novels

The Immortal Gene (Book One)
The Immortal Target (Book Two)

Standalone Novels

'Til Death Do Us Part
The Drowning
The Woman in the Woods
The Threat
The Specter
The Mafia Trilogy
A Murder in Time
Frequency of the Dead

Co-Authored Novels

Collision Course (Written with Gary Ponzo)
There Will Be Blood (Written with Rania Stone)
The Soulless (Written with Rania Stone)

Short Story Collections

Twisted Fate (Tales of Horror)
Twists of Fate (Tales of Hope)

Chapter 1

Sarah Roberts stared at her watch. It was 10:15 a.m.

Only three minutes left until the precognition came true. Only three minutes until someone died—or she saved them.

She found a few stray hairs above the nape of her neck. She massaged them between her fingers until they were firmly in her grip, then tugged them out. Eyes closed, she leaned back on the dirty concrete and savored the calming moment. The sharp pain crawling over her skin soothed her and relaxed her nerves.

The next time she had to wait under a bridge for whatever was supposed to happen, she would bring a pillow to sit on. The section of concrete she crouched on angled down toward a small river at forty-five degrees. The grass on either side looked more comfortable, but the message had been specific. If there was anything Sarah knew, it was to follow the instructions with absolute precision.

Sit directly in the middle, under the St. Elizabeth Bridge. 10:18 a.m. Bring hammer.

Bring hammer?

The hammer sat beside her on the concrete with no apparent purpose.

She rechecked the time.

10:17 a.m.

Some of the remaining hair on her forearm stood as a chill coursed through her. Within one minute, something was going to happen. This heightened state of awareness always made what hair she had left rise in anticipation of what was to come. It also showed Sarah the location of more hair to be pulled later.

She picked up the hammer.

Her pulse quickened as vehicles crossed the bridge above her, engines revving. She looked down at her feet, where a pile of cigarette butts was scattered from previous occupants who had loitered under the bridge.

She focused on her breathing.

Keep it regular, she thought, exhaling slowly. *Just wait for it.*

A dead-fish smell wafted up from the river.

The water made a soft, spinning, whooshing sound. At any other time, the sound would have been soothing.

Cars continued to cruise over the bridge above. Something louder, a semi-truck maybe, came and went.

She glanced at her watch one last time.

10:18 a.m.

Here we go ...

A tire screeched. A horn blared. The sound of metal hitting metal was surreal. It made her jump as she involuntarily covered her head with her arms for protection. Another set of tires squealed before splintering wood and crunching metal signaled that the guardrail had been hit.

A vehicle came into view at an impossible angle. It fell toward the river, along with pieces of the guardrail. The car hit the water roof first and wallowed upside down, the passenger side canted slightly upward.

Sarah scrambled down the embankment and reached the car in seconds. She knelt and peered through the window on the driver's side. A woman who looked to be in her twenties was trapped in the seat belt. She was inverted, her arms dangling toward the water that was slipping in where it could. A small line of blood trickled down her forehead into her hairline. She appeared to be unconscious. A quick inspection of the vehicle showed Sarah there were no passengers.

The river was relatively shallow in this area—it rushed by just below Sarah's knees—but it was high enough to cover the driver's head. An odd thought struck her. *Why didn't the precognition say anything about proper footwear for wading through water? Mom's going to be pissed that I soaked my new shoes.*

Sarah grabbed the handle and tried to open the door. It didn't move. She pushed the back door. It was also stuck or locked. She looked across to the other side of the car. The doors on that side were bent inward. That was the side that hit the river first, buckling it.

Her stomach churned when she looked at the woman. The water had risen to her hairline and was swirling around the top of her head.

Time was running out.

People yelled from the bridge behind her asking if everyone was okay.

Water was now touching the woman's eyebrows.

The hammer.

She looked at the hammer in her hand. If she bashed the driver's side window in, it would shatter and could hurt the woman. She would have to enter through the back door window.

She raised the hammer and whacked the pane.

Nothing happened.

She snuck a peek at the woman. Her eyes were submerged now. Sarah guessed she had less than a minute before the woman's nose started taking water on.

She swung back farther, twisting with her hips, and shouted as she whacked the window. The back pane shattered and blew inward. She used the hammer to remove stray pieces of glass still attached to the door frame.

The water had grown tolerable as she had stood in it but made her gasp when she dropped down on all fours. She crawled as fast as she could into the back seat while trying to keep from being cut by the remaining shards of glass.

Items from inside the car floated and bobbed in the water around her. She brushed them aside while reaching for the woman.

From the back, she angled herself between the front seats. She lifted the woman's head just as the water flirted with her nostrils.

That was where she was stopped.

Sarah reasoned it would be difficult to undo the seatbelt that suspended the driver. How could she push or drag her from the car? It would be impossible for Sarah alone, especially since she couldn't go through the driver's side door.

She would have to stay here, leaning on her side, holding the woman's head up against her shoulder. She used her free hand to cling to the steering wheel.

The water level inside the car matched the outside now.

Until help arrived, she had done all she could do. It was over.

Minutes later, sirens wailed in the distance.

And not soon enough, she thought.

Her adrenaline rush was ebbing, and the shivering had started. With her strength diminishing, Sarah held the woman's head above the water until the firemen reached the river. They cut the driver's side door off and removed the woman's seatbelt, lifting the driver out.

Another fireman reached in and helped Sarah from the car and up to the top of the bridge. A paramedic provided a blanket for her. She sat on the bumper of an ambulance as an officer fired questions at her. Had she been a passenger? Did she see the accident? How was she involved? As before, in situations like these, she was evasive. She hated cops, even the sight of them. She told the police officer she would answer his questions after she warmed up.

Paramedics were attending to people in a minivan where a man in the driver's seat was being fitted with a neck brace. A garbage truck had lost one of its wheels which looked to be the cause of the accident.

In the confusion of people, some hurt, some helping, Sarah dropped the blanket and disappeared behind the ambulance. She removed the red bandanna she wore to cover her missing hair. She never wanted to be identified as the girl with no eyebrows and hardly any hair on her head. Without the bandanna, she would stand out a lot more.

She started running. She had to get home before her mother began asking where she had been.

She hated having to lie to her.

Chapter 2

THE NEXT MORNING, SARAH had a new mission. She had woken to a note on her bedroom floor that said: *Dolan. Save yourself.* On the back of the note were instructions for Sarah to go to the psychic fair in town to find him.

The ominous message frightened her.

Save yourself.

Was this a reference to her, or was she supposed to tell Dolan to save himself?

Sarah paid her fee at the main desk, pushed through the doors, and entered the psychic fair. The room was packed full of people, each person waiting their turn at one of the dozens of booths. Psychics and fortune tellers were dispersed throughout the room in rows. Some of the psychic peddlers were seated in actual booths; others merely had a table with a crystal ball resting on an intricately designed base with two chairs tucked against the table.

Why am I here?

She clutched her notebook against her chest and held it tight. Within four strides, she was around an aisle corner and hustling down through a crowd.

She smelled something strange. Soft music, trancelike, issued from small speakers on a table to her left. She moved on, lost, with no direction, only purpose.

Sarah adjusted and tightened her bandanna. She couldn't risk it loosening and falling off in public; people would stare and be horrified by her missing hair. Six months earlier, she had been diagnosed with a condition called *trichotillomania*. The doctor described it as an impulsive control disorder where Sarah needed to pull her hair out. He had tried to explain it to her mother by saying Sarah was a puller instead of a cutter. She remembered her mother flipping out when she realized that all the missing hair was Sarah's fault—she doubted her mother even heard the *"but at least she's not self-mutilating with razor blades"* consolation the doctor had offered.

Her nose was clogged with the smell of incense. She moved on down the aisle, anxiety twisting her insides. Men walked past her every few seconds. She could not start asking if they were this guy Dolan. She didn't want the attention.

Why do I have to get these messages anyway?

A bell sounded somewhere in the building. She felt people staring. Maybe it was her missing eyebrows drawing their attention.

Oh man, why am I here, she thought again. *I am nothing like these people. I'm different. I'm real. What happens to me is not the same as what these fake psychics are doing.*

She turned to leave. She made it three steps before someone grabbed her arm. Sarah jumped and snapped around.

"Hold up there, young lady."

"What's up?" she asked, angry at being startled.

"I know *what* you are."

The old woman who grabbed her had the classic look of a fortuneteller, like an old gypsy, with a headband and wrinkly skin. Her confidence was evident in her posture; this woman had spent many years offering a glimpse of the future for a dollar.

"What do you write in that notebook?" the old woman asked.

"What are you talking about?" Sarah stepped back from the woman, trying to use her body to shield the notebook. She allowed no one access to it.

"Come back to my booth where we can talk."

"Forget it," Sarah said, feeling spooked. "I'm done with this place." Sarah started to walk away. She had barely made a move before a revelation occurred to her. She turned to look back at the old woman. "What did you mean when you said you know *what* I am?"

"Come back to my booth. I'll tell you there." The old woman turned away and gestured with her arm in a beckoning motion. "I've got a message for you."

A message?

Sarah decided to follow her, but not out of curiosity. She followed her because it was rare that someone didn't stare at her missing eyebrows. This woman held her gaze as she talked. Sarah followed out of respect.

The old woman shooed away a few people who huddled around her table and gestured for Sarah to sit. In the center of the woman's booth sat a table with a crystal ball. However, the booth was open so anyone could eavesdrop on their conversation. Luckily most people were there for their own personal benefit and did not care to listen in on the possible future of others.

Sarah did her best to assume control of the situation. "Before we talk, I want to know how much you'll charge when *you* invited *me*."

"No charge." The woman raised her hand in protest. "My name is Esmerelda. I know what you are, and you have to stop."

"What am I?" Sarah pretended to be bored.

"You write things in that notebook. Whatever it is, I feel you act on or alter your routine because of it."

How could this woman know that unless she really is psychic?

Sarah bent forward as her stomach knotted. The fear in what she did when answering her precognitions was nothing compared to being found out.

She hadn't come here to be discovered.

"I want to see your notebook." The old woman held her hand out, waiting for Sarah to give her the sacred journal.

Sarah tightened her grip on it. Her palms were becoming sweaty, just like every other time she felt a blackout coming on.

"Never." She leaned back in her chair. "No one sees what's in here." She looked around the booth. She needed to leave. First, she had to find out if this woman could help with the original reason she came to the fair today.

"Do you know a man named Dolan?" Sarah blurted as she moved to the edge of her seat.

The old woman's eyes narrowed. "Why did you say that name? Is it in your notebook? I need to see it because I'm one of the real ones and I can see you're in a lot of danger. I might be able to help."

It came out so easily—a warning of danger.

"What danger?" Sarah asked.

The woman leaned forward in her chair and began to get up. Sarah noticed how long the woman's earrings were and wondered how her flesh still held them. They were red dangling things that rested on her shoulders. Heavy earrings had long since made this woman's lobe look like Sarah's little finger.

"You're in danger. It'll happen within twenty-four hours. I've seen people like your kind before." The old woman was standing now, her face turning nearly the same shade of red as her earrings. "You're an automatic writer, just like me. You receive messages from the Other Side. That's why I need to see what's in your notebook. Then I'll be able to tell you about the danger you face because I wrote down that I'd meet you here today. I wrote that I would meet one of my kind, and she would look just like you."

"Why are you talking in circles?" Sarah asked. "Tell me about the danger."

"You have a gift," the woman said. "Use it wisely."

"Hold up. When you told me about danger, were you threatening me or talking about my *gift*?"

"Sarah, whatever message is in your notebook, I think it's a message for you. I think you need to save yourself."

Sarah shuddered. *Save yourself. And how did this woman know my name?*

Fear almost paralyzed her.

Sarah looked down at her hand. It started to twitch.

Oh no. Not here.

Her hand twitched again, this time with more urgency.

Breathing became an effort.

She stood, hopped over the railing on her right, and ran down an aisle leading through a crowded area to the main doors.

She looked back.

No one was following her.

If what that woman said was true, trouble was coming, and it would be here soon. She felt very alone in a pavilion that was filled with people.

Two men stood in her way at the doors. She was not able to get around them fast enough. Her balance was lost in her panic. She bent over and hit the floor.

She felt the familiar signs of a total blackout as her vision closed down.

Someone asked if she was okay. She opened her eyes and immediately went for her notebook.

It was gone.

Her pen rested on the floor beside her.

She made to get to her feet, her eyes scanning the ground around her for the notebook in a panic.

"I was asking if you were okay."

She looked up to see an older, distinguished-looking man staring down at her.

"I'm fine." Sarah picked up her pen.

"You appeared to blackout or something. You scribbled in your notebook, and then … are you sure you're okay?"

The man glared at her. For some unknown reason, he appeared upset. His voice contradicted his eyes. Some of her resolve came back. She regained her footing and, along with that, some of her tenacity.

"I'm fine," Sarah repeated. "Where is my notebook?"

"Let me introduce myself. I'm the president of the psychic fair. My name is Dolan Ryan."

Dolan.

In the flesh.

She couldn't believe it. Here he was, the man she was supposed to see, but her notebook was gone.

"Do you have my notebook?"

"No. I was talking to my assistant when you bumped into us and fell. I saw you writing in it. Then you got up. I'm sorry, but I don't see it anymore."

If her notebook fell into the wrong hands, or the hands of *anyone* for that matter, Sarah was done for. It held information about the last six months of accidents and crimes she witnessed and stopped: a beating, the kidnapping of Mary Bennett, car accidents.

It felt like the pavilion suddenly grew darker, smaller.

Was this the danger she was in? Would the police get her notebook and want to talk to her?

She backed away from Dolan. With a glance to her right, she saw the old woman, Esmerelda, watching her.

Her parents walked up.

"Sarah, there you are. We're here to pick you up. Are you done yet?"

She turned toward them and almost hugged her mother. The look on

Sarah's face must have been apparent.

"Honey, what's wrong? Are you okay?"

Sarah held up a finger for her mother to wait and moved back toward Dolan.

The tension in the air was palpable.

Speaking loud enough for only Dolan to hear, she said, "I was sent here to give you a message: *Save yourself.*"

A minute later, heading away from Dolan toward the open pavilion doors, her mother asked, "What was that all about? Who were that man and the old woman staring at you?"

"I'll tell you on the way home," Sarah said.

Sarah ran from the building without her notebook, her parents trailing behind, her father strangely quiet.

Sarah left the psychic fair, still unsure if the message '*save yourself*' was actually meant for her.

Chapter 3

Sarah should never have come here, Esmerelda thought.

The fair had closed twenty minutes ago. The area she stood in was dark except for a few random night lights. There was just enough illumination for her to see which way to walk out to her trailer in the back.

The last piece to stow away was her crystal ball, the one prop she hated the most because of how fake it was. To have someone with her talents using such a prop seemed disrespectful. It was all for show; everything was for show. That was how the public had to see it, as per Dolan.

"Esmerelda."

She jumped, almost dropping the crystal ball. Before speaking, she turned and set the ball back down on the table.

"What do you want?" Something was wrong. He didn't seem himself.

"You look jittery," Dolan said, a half-smile playing across his lips. "It's not usual for you. If I had to guess, I'd say something's bothering you."

Esmerelda put her hands out in front of her, palms facing him. "Don't try to use psychic stuff on me, Dolan."

"I'm not. You know my rules on that. I never use my gifts against fellow psychics."

She stepped back. Dolan walked around her booth table and sat in the customer's chair.

"I came over because I wanted to talk to you about a customer you had today. I would've come sooner but had to eliminate all the naggers."

"Naggers? Is that what you call the public?" Esmerelda didn't sit. She leaned back against a steel post bordering her booth.

"No, not in general. I had to give a name to the stragglers. They remind me of the paparazzi."

"Who can resist you?" she asked, trying not to sound too sarcastic.

"Esmerelda, you've been with the fair for a long time. We've known each other for over twenty years. Why do I hear bitterness in your voice?"

Esmerelda looked away. Dolan was right. Why was she feeling disrupted? Maybe because she knew Sarah was so young and she was playing a game unaware of its rules. She should have stopped Sarah earlier. She should have taken her by the arm and told her exactly how much danger she was in. She should have told her to stop listening to the messages in her notebook.

"I'm sorry, Dolan. You're right. It's been a long day."

"Do you remember the young girl with the missing hair? Quite a distinguishing feature, don't you think?"

"I recall her. Why do you ask?" She had no idea why Dolan would be interested in Sarah.

"I bumped into her after she left your booth."

Esmerelda could feel his gaze on her. Did Dolan recognize Sarah for what she was?

"I saw the incident. If you're looking to apologize to her, it's too late. I don't keep personal records of the people I read for, but you already know that. Actually, I didn't even get the chance to do a reading for her." Esmerelda turned and met Dolan's eyes. "Is there something you're not telling me?"

"Look, Esmerelda. I'm not sure what it is myself. I felt some kind of spark with that girl. She had a message in her notebook. I have no idea what it means, but it's quite unsettling."

Dolan lowered his head. Esmerelda waited for him to continue.

In the seconds of silence between them, she heard someone walking nearby. She edged her head out of her booth and looked down the aisle to see a suit jacket flutter past a booth about six down from hers. A black jacket … the same one Alex wore, Dolan's assistant, earlier today. Was the assistant listening in or coincidentally walking by? She lifted her nose and took a deep breath to see if she could detect his cologne.

"Did you hear that?" she asked.

"Hear what?"

Esmerelda brushed it off with her hand and gestured for Dolan to continue. "You said there was something else?"

"Yes."

He got up from the chair and looked down at Esmerelda. She was almost two feet shorter than him.

"She had a notebook with her. When she fell to the floor, it popped open. I went to help her, but she fell into a trance and wrote something down. Then she snapped out of it."

Esmerelda waited for Dolan to go on. In the darkened pavilion, she hadn't noticed how anxious he looked. This was more serious than she had initially thought.

"I saw *my* name in her notebook. She circled it numerous times before getting to her feet. There were two words beside it."

"Having your name in her notebook shouldn't be a mystery. You're the one that makes this psychic fair popular. Everyone comes to see you. After all the help you've given the police with missing person cases, you're a celebrity."

Dolan shook his head as if he was frustrated. "By my name, it said, 'save yourself.'"

Esmerelda sat down. "Sarah is an automatic writer. The problem is she's changing the future. She's getting precognitions about people needing help and then attempting to help them."

"How do you know all this? You read that much?"

"No, I recognized her from the news. She saved a woman from drowning under the St. Elizabeth Bridge, the anchorwoman who crashed over the edge and ended up in the water when that garbage truck lost its wheel."

"That was this girl, Sarah?"

"Yes, and she is in trouble. Something's coming, but I couldn't tell what. She needs help. As soon as I told her she needed help, she bolted. I wish I could do more, but I fear that—within twenty-four hours—Sarah will either be dead or a victim of whatever incident she's trying to prevent."

Chapter 4

Sarah couldn't believe what was happening. She lay on her bed, not sure what move to make.

When she met Esmerelda at the psychic fair yesterday, all she got was a warning. Sarah's parents had argued most of the night about her.

The thought of the danger supposedly coming created mounting pressure. Maybe it had to do with her notebook. If the police ever got their hands on it, she would have some explaining to do—the kind of explaining that got you locked up with a lovely white jacket.

Automatic writer? She had no idea what that was. Thinking back to her short conversation with Esmerelda, she could come to only one conclusion.

Someone or something from the Other Side was using her as a tool.

She needed to get her notebook back. She wanted to reread all the entries and then destroy them.

She could not turn to her parents. It would only fuel their current arguments. She felt guilty enough for that. They wouldn't listen anyway. They always treated her like a child. Even now, at eighteen years old, they still treated her like she needed to be sheltered. Some of it was her fault. She hadn't moved out yet, and there was no indication that she would any time soon.

She had no friends to speak of. She knew people from school but had no real friends she could trust. She had no boyfriend. Who would want one anyway? With all the trouble a relationship seemed to be, adding one to her mixed-up situation would be the last thing she needed.

She would have to see Esmerelda again. Maybe she could properly explain what automatic writing was to her.

She got up and sat on the edge of her bed.

Was Dolan in trouble? Could she help? If she could, why weren't the messages she received more specific?

Should she help?

Sarah picked up her bedroom phone. After dialing information, she was connected to the psychic fair's number. On the third ring, a woman picked it up.

Sarah could feel her hand shaking from the phone's vibration against her ear. She was taken aback by this because she had been in situations in the last six months that should have scared her more than dealing with this.

But this one felt more personal, more dangerous. Suddenly, the *save yourself* message seemed to be aimed at Sarah.

She asked the woman who answered the phone for Esmerelda and was told she was in a session and couldn't be disturbed. Sarah left her name and telephone number and hung up.

She grabbed her address book and opened it to an entry she had made months ago about Mary Bennett, who turned out to be the daughter of a wealthy family. There had been an attempted kidnapping, and—at the right moment—Sarah had stepped in and stopped it. After Mary was confirmed to be okay, Sarah tried to slink away undetected, but she was stopped by Mary, who had written her phone number down and told Sarah to call if she needed anything. Anything at all.

Sarah dialed the number Mary had given her all those months ago. A male, probably a servant, answered and told Sarah to hold while he went to find Mary.

A moment later, a female voice came on the line.

"Hello, who's this?"

Sarah recognized Mary's voice. She would never forget it; Mary had been her first save.

"It's Sarah," she whispered.

"Sarah? I don't know any Sarahs—oh, wait. Are you the girl with no eyebrows, the one who was by the trash bin that night?"

"Yes."

"Hold on. I want to talk to you, but not here. Let me put the phone down so I can go to my room. You'll wait?"

"Yes, I'll wait."

Sarah heard the phone drop and feet shuffling. Moments later, she heard the familiar click of a phone lifting and Mary yelling that she got it. The other line was put down.

"Why haven't you called sooner? I've got so many questions."

"I like to stay anonymous. I don't make it a practice to get to know the people I help."

"Are you saying I'm not the only one you've helped? Is this something you do regularly?" Mary sounded surprised and delighted.

"Not regularly. Only when I'm supposed to." Sarah stood and moved to her bedroom window. Her parents were still out, so she didn't have to worry about them overhearing anything. "Listen, I didn't call to talk about that. I wanted to ask for your help."

"Help? Whatever it is, I'll give it my best. Shoot."

"I need you to do two simple tasks for me. It involves my father and a woman named Esmerelda."

Chapter 5

Esmerelda spent the next day trying to figure out what was bothering her more. Could she be *that* concerned about Sarah, a girl she had just met? Or was it what Dolan had said last night?

She reached around and grabbed the closed sign, flipping it. She was done for the day. No more clients, no more brooding. She placed it in its holder on the table.

"Closing early?"

The voice startled her. Dolan's assistant stepped into view. She should have sniffed him coming. He was always doused in cologne.

"Yes. I'm not feeling well. I wouldn't be at my best for the clientele."

"But it's only the lunch hour. Do you feel Dolan will approve of his top psychic taking off early?"

"I don't care what Dolan approves of. I should've retired years ago. I do this because I want to. I don't work for you or Dolan."

"All right, all right, you needn't get so defensive. I was merely concerned about your well-being."

Yeah, right, she thought. She wondered why she always felt the need to explain herself to Alex. Why did she even talk to him? Not many of the employees got along with him. Some of the lunchroom talk was curiosity about why Dolan kept him on.

"I'm leaving, Alex. I'll be back tomorrow."

"Where are you going?"

"It's none of your business. But if you must know, I'm going to my trailer for a siesta."

Esmerelda edged her way around the booth's table. The closer she got to Alex, the more intense his cologne was. Suffocating, like it seared the oxygen out of the air.

She expected Alex to say something within two steps, but he remained quiet. Esmerelda walked away in silence.

It was a slow day at the fair anyway. She'd only had a few people to read for this morning, and as she walked through the pavilion, she could see it was half empty.

When she reached the back exit door, she stopped at the sight of Dolan.

"Where're you going, Esmerelda?"

"To my trailer, Dolan."

He moved in front of the back door, his arms crossed.

"I want to talk to you about that girl you did a reading for yesterday."

"Again? We discussed her last night. I know nothing more."

"Ah, but I think you do. Come with me."

She had no intention of going anywhere with him.

She moved for the exit door, but Dolan reached out and gripped her arm above the elbow. He led her away from the back door.

"Hey, what are you doing? Let go of me."

"We need to talk."

It was so unlike Dolan to act this way, so uncharacteristic. Maybe her precognition of danger had come true, and Sarah's parents were here demanding answers.

Minutes later, they were under a steel staircase that led to the offices above. The closest booth or fair attendee was at least thirty feet away.

"Alex and I were having a conversation yesterday when we bumped into Sarah," Dolan started. "You already know what I saw in her notebook. Alex is curious about it, too. I remember you said that Sarah could be dead or a victim of one of her own precognitions. But that only works with *'save yourself.'* So tell me, what's going on? Should I be worried?" Dolan ran a finger through his hair, obviously anxious. "I mean, yesterday, just before she leaves the pavilion, she whispers that I need to save myself. But then you tell me she is the victim. Is this about Sarah or me?"

"I told you yesterday I didn't even get a chance to do a full reading." This was so unlike Dolan. "Why did you drag me over here to ask the same questions from last night? What are you worried about?"

"It's got me freaked out."

She saw something in Dolan's eyes that didn't seem right. The fair was still quite empty. No one was close enough to hear them. Esmerelda stepped back.

Dolan said, "Alex was standing by your booth when he overheard you say the girl was in danger. Alex listened in a little more. Esmerelda, you know it isn't the practice of Dolan Ryan's psychic fair to do negative readings. I not only want to know what you were talking about, but I also need to know if it relates to me."

"I'm sorry, Dolan, but I refuse to talk about it. As far as I'm concerned, it has nothing to do with you."

She could see his surprise. He took a step back.

"Whatever Alex heard," Esmerelda continued, "wasn't meant for his ears or yours. The reading was for Sarah and Sarah alone. I can't tell you about the danger because I don't know what it is."

"Esmerelda, how long have we been at this together, doing readings, helping people find love, marriage, peace? You, of all people, know me. As the years have been getting tougher and tougher, I want to make a little more money and then get away from all this. I'm done, Esmerelda. I want obscurity. Please, tell me what's going on. Was the *save yourself* warning meant for her and not me?"

"I have nothing further to say about this. I didn't get to see inside her notebook."

Esmerelda turned to leave, but Dolan stopped her.

"What's happening to you, Dolan? I have never seen you like this."

"I need to know why you won't talk to me. Is this girl's problem related to me? Tell me, Esmerelda."

She kept her mouth closed.

"Esmerelda?"

His jaw clenched when he said her name. She felt his anger, his desperation.

She stepped back and walked away in a half-jog. Their impromptu meeting was over. The truth was, she really didn't know what form the danger would take. One thing was it did have something to do with the psychic fair, and she wanted no part of that.

On her way out the back door, she saw Alex again. He was sitting on the table in her booth, watching her.

Chapter 6

Sarah sat near the exit doors at the rear of the bus. It was empty but for a few teenagers. The doors rattled shut, and the bus lumbered forward.

After she had talked to Mary Bennett, Sarah felt she had made a mistake. Trusting people had always been a big deal for her, and now she realized she'd probably said too much to Mary.

They seemed to have had a mutual connection on the phone, which made Sarah feel odd because they had only talked once before. This was new for her. Sarah wasn't used to having to rely on other people.

Mary said the reason she wanted to help was because *of* Sarah. Not only had Sarah saved her from being kidnapped, but she also intrigued her. Mary said her life was boring, whereas Sarah's life sounded exciting. She wanted to get involved the next time Sarah went to stop a kidnapping. Sarah brushed that off and secured Mary's commitment to helping in exactly the way Sarah needed her to and then got off the phone.

The familiar *ding* of pressing the "next stop" button made her jump and woke her from her reverie just in time. She was a block from the pavilion where the psychic fair was held.

Once off the bus, she headed to the front entrance, where a registration table sat with two women perched behind it.

She realized too late she did not have enough money to cover the entry fee for the fair. She thought about asking if a notebook had been returned to lost and found but then thought better of it.

Talk to Esmerelda first, she thought.

"I would like to get a message to Esmerelda, a reader here at the fair," she said to the desk attendees.

One of the women, with a smile that showed all her teeth and some of her gums, looked up at her. "What would you like me to pass along?"

"Could you tell her that Sarah Roberts is out front and I would like to talk to her? Tell her that it concerns the reading she did for me yesterday."

"I could, but I don't think she'll be able to drop what she's doing to come out front. She's one of the most popular psychics we have here. She's probably got a line at her booth right now. But I'll make sure she gets the message."

"Thank you." Sarah grabbed a pen and paper from the table. She wrote down her home phone number. If she couldn't meet with her, at least Esmerelda could call.

She set the paper down on the table along with the pen. Both women ignored her, chatting with each other. Neither attempted to deliver her note.

She needed to find another way in.

Sarah stepped outside and headed along the edge of the building. She turned the corner to find the back lot, which consisted of a fenced-in yard with a security shack. The yard was cluttered with roughly a dozen trailers and rigs. It looked to Sarah that the psychics lived in the trailers while on the road, moving from location to location.

The sun shone bright, bouncing off the pavement in a wave of heat. She backhanded sweat from her brow and started for the fence.

As she passed an emergency exit door, she pulled on it. It was locked from the inside.

There appeared to be no way into the building unless she could get through the fenced-in area.

The security shack was manned, but the guard had his head down and appeared to be reading something.

Sarah walked up to the fence. She looked at the guard shack. The guard's head was still down.

She started to climb. It took her less than ten seconds to reach the top. Straddling the bar, she adjusted her weight and began descending to the other side. With three feet to go, she hopped off and looked at the guard shack again. The security guard hadn't seen a thing. She tightened her bandanna, adjusted her clothes, then headed toward the trailers.

"Hey! You there!"

Sarah swung to the right and saw a man in a sports jacket coming her way. She looked back at the guard's shack and saw the guard coming out, a scowl on his face.

Then her hand twitched. *Oh no, not now.*

She felt light-headed. As she blacked out and fell to the pavement, Sarah banged against the fence.

When she came to, the man in the sports jacket was kneeling beside her, trying to pry her new notepad out of her hands. She held tight, twisting her body away for leverage. The notepad popped out of the guy's hands.

The security guard yelled from his shack that the police were around the corner.

Sarah opened the pad and turned away so no one could see what was written on its pages.

Her precognition was on the first page.

"The police?" Sarah asked, turning back around to face the security guard.

"Yes," the man with the sports jacket said. "You're trespassing. But I'd be willing to drop the charges if you told me what you wrote in that notepad."

Sarah slid the notepad into the back of her pants. She looked away without a word and walked toward the guard shack, where the guard was busy unlocking the padlock to the gate.

"I need to speak to Esmerelda. That's why I'm here."

The guard looked past her to the man in the sports jacket. "All readings are done in the pavilion. The front entrance is how you get access to the psychics. What you have done is called breaking and entering. You can discuss it with the cops."

Sarah saw a cruiser pulling up outside the fence, and her stomach dropped. She detested cops at the best of times.

The gate had rolled open, and Sport Jacket was now talking to the police.

Minutes later, Sarah was put into the back seat of the cruiser.

Both officers got in the front after a five-minute wait.

As they exited the lot, Sarah looked out the back window and saw Esmerelda running to the gate. Sarah waved, knowing Esmerelda could see her.

She wondered what Esmerelda would think of her being taken away in a police car. Maybe this was the extent of the danger she had foretold?

The driver asked where she lived and headed in that direction. They explained that this would be a warning. The next time she was found inside the property of the pavilion without being a paying customer, she would be charged with trespassing and have a criminal record.

She nodded her understanding. She found stray hairs on her forearm and yanked them out hard. The rush was instant, cooling, calming her.

When they got to her house, her mother came out to meet them. The police recited a quick rundown of what had happened and let Sarah out of the back seat into *the custody of her parents*, as they put it.

She could see how furious her mother was, but Sarah ignored her and ran to her bedroom. She retrieved the note from the notepad and read it. This time, there were two messages.

The first one told her more about Dolan and what she needed to do for him. The second entry read: *Tonight. 9:23 p.m. Birk Street. North Face. Kidnapping.*

She did what the note asked her to do for Dolan.

When she was done, she sat on her bed, her insides tingling with excitement.

What would Dolan think when he found the note she was leaving for him?

This was the first time real names had come through.

It was especially unsettling since it involved crimes being committed and not just accidents.

What would the police do with information like this?

She just hoped she could count on Mary Bennett to come through for her.

Chapter 7

HER MOTHER'S FOOTSTEPS POUNDED down the hall. Sarah fumbled with the note she had written about the kidnapping. She tucked it into her back pocket as her bedroom door flew open.

"What the hell was that all about?" her mother asked, obviously angry. "They found you trespassing at the psychic fair? What's going on, Sarah? You didn't even want to go yesterday. What were you doing there again today?"

Sarah remained silent. She kept her eyes aimed at the carpet.

"Sarah, I won't ask you again."

She looked up and saw her mother standing in the doorway, arms crossed, anger contorting her face.

"I went to see Esmerelda—"

"Why? Wasn't yesterday enough? And where would you get the money? Don't tell me this has anything to do with your blackouts because we all know how obsessive you can get. Just look at your hair or what's left of it."

That was not fair. Already the conversation was turning into insults. She didn't like confrontations with her mother. She never won them.

The edge of her bed was a good place to sit and wait for this ordeal to be over.

"I'm sorry, that was uncalled for." Her mother uncrossed her arms and turned her expression into one of feigned concern. "Look, I want your notebook."

Sarah's heart sank. She didn't have it, but since she never went anywhere without it, there was no way her mother would believe that. She only had the new one from today. Her mother had never wanted anything to do with it before. What had changed?

She tried hard to keep her eyes downcast. Her mother usually read too much in them.

"I said I want your notebook, and I want it now." She marched toward the bed.

Sarah flinched away. "I don't have it."

"What do you mean you don't have it? Don't lie to me." Her mother's eyes narrowed. She leaned forward, coming within a foot of Sarah's face. "You are going to give me your notebook. This is not open for discussion. Do you understand me?"

Sarah nodded. She didn't want to say anything more that might spin her mother into a tantrum. She hated it when her mother flew off the handle, and right now, she wasn't sure what she was capable of.

"Get off that bed and get me your notebook. I know you know where it is because it's never out of your sight for long. If you've lost it, find it. Now!"

Sarah stood and moved to her night table. She opened drawers, looked under her pillow, opened her closet, and moved clothes around.

"What're you doing?" her mother asked. "Stop wasting time, and just give me your notebook."

"I am looking for it. Why do you want it anyway? You never showed interest before."

"I talked to Mary," her mother said calmly.

Sarah's stomach dropped further. Her right hand reached up to her neck and grabbed her hair.

She pulled. The pain was quick and intense. Comfort warmed her; adrenaline filled her stomach.

Why would they talk?

"She called me. I hung up just before the police pulled in with you."

"What did she tell you?" Sarah asked.

"Everything."

Her mother was being evasive on purpose. Sarah guessed she didn't know much after all. This was a fishing expedition.

"What's everything?" Heat rose to her cheeks.

"Find your notebook, and we will discuss it. I know that Mary will be in one of your entries."

Her mother *did* know more than she was letting on. That also confirmed how much of a mistake it had been to talk to Mary.

Sarah felt lightheaded, her knees weak. She would not give the notebook up to anyone, even if she had it.

But how was she to handle her mom? She continued to pretend to look. She opened more drawers, looked under clothes, and even lifted the top mattress to look between the two.

She realized the only way out of this might have to be physical. She felt the pit in her stomach getting heavier.

There was another kidnap victim she had to help tonight. Nothing would stop her from being there.

The police are useless. It has to be me.

She had never forgiven herself for letting Kim Wepps get taken after her kidnapping details were found in the notebook. She remembered reading about Kim Wepps in the newspaper the day after she hadn't helped her.

"I'd give it to you if I could find it. I looked for it this morning and haven't seen it since."

It was weak. She wondered if her mother would know she was lying by the cracking in her voice.

"Come on, Sarah, that little book is never far from your grasp."

Sarah crossed her arms. "Tell me what Mary said to you."

"She wanted to know where you were. She asked if you were the one who saved that television woman."

"What television woman?" she asked, acting naïve.

"You know, that accident where the famous anchorwoman for NBC was hit by a truck and knocked off a bridge. Her car landed upside down in a river. Apparently, a girl jumped in and saved the newswoman from drowning while she was still unconscious. Then the teenager disappeared. After I talked to Mary, I went down to your dad's toolbox, and I couldn't find his hammer."

"Why would you look for Dad's hammer?" Sarah asked, feeling nervous at being found out even though she'd done nothing wrong.

"The news said the teenage girl broke out the back window of the woman's car with a hammer. The police are looking for this mysterious helper. They had some questions that went unanswered. I told Mary that it was impossible you were involved, but she went on about your notebook and how you saved her from a kidnapping. Not only that, she said you called her earlier. To tell you the truth, Mary was surprised that I had no idea what she was talking about. That's why I have to have your notebook. I need to see the kind of things you write in it."

Sarah tried to keep the conversation flowing. The last thing she wanted was for her mother to detect her nervousness. "That's so strange. I've never been involved in *kidnappings* or anything like that."

The shrill ring from the phone made her jump.

"Are you expecting a call?" her mother asked.

Sarah shook her head. "If I was expecting a call, wouldn't it ring on my line in my bedroom?"

She followed her mother into her father's den, her pulse racing, hoping it wasn't Mary again. Her mother picked it up on the fourth ring.

"Hello?" She looked up at Sarah. "Yes, she's here. Hold on, please." She placed her palm over the mouthpiece and whispered to Sarah, "It's someone from that psychic fair."

Sarah lunged for the phone. Her mother pulled it away.

"How dare you!" She scowled down at Sarah. "Who is this, and how did this man get our number? And why is he calling for you?"

"I have no idea," Sarah said as she reached for the phone again, snatching it from her mother's grasp.

"Hello," Sarah said, moving away from her mother to lean against the wall by the window.

"Who I am isn't important," a man said, his voice deep. "All you need to know is that I saw you today at the psychic fair. I want to help. But before I can do that, I need to meet with you. You will have to bring your notebook."

Focus, she thought.

"Yes, I understand," she said.

The hand holding the phone twitched. It felt like the beginning of a blackout, yet not strong enough.

"Good. How about you come back to the fair and ask for …"

Pain shot through her hand, starting at the elbow. She fumbled and almost dropped the phone. "Of course. That would be no problem. Goodbye." She hung up without hearing the name.

"What was that all about?" her mother asked, arms crossed over her chest again.

"I can't tell you," Sarah replied. She needed to be defiant and take a stand.

"*What?* Why not?" The look of surprise was genuine.

"Because the caller asked for confidentiality."

"You *can* tell me who you're going to meet and where. You can tell me *why,* too."

Sarah shrugged, trying to downplay the situation. "Sorry, this is between me and the psychic fair."

Her mother's finger was raised and poised in front of Sarah's nose, pointing close enough to cause Sarah's eyes to cross. "Listen to me, *little* girl. You *will* tell me what's going on. I need to know what you've been up to?"

"I don't think so." Sarah turned away. She mustered up every bit of boldness she had inside of her. "You want to know what your problem is, Mother?" She had never talked to her mother with such a disrespectful tone. She couldn't look her in the eyes. "You still think you have a parent-to-child relationship with me, and that has to change. I'm going to be nineteen soon. We are now in an adult-to-adult relationship." She walked away and shouted over her shoulder. "I'm going to meet Mary."

"I can't believe this," her mother bellowed, hands flying up from her sides. "Are you taking lessons from your father? You listen to me. You will tell me what I want to know because I'm your mother—"

Sarah ran down the stairs to the front door, knowing what would happen if her mother tried to stop her and regretting the confrontation in advance.

After leaving the house, she walked the length of the driveway as the sun faded beneath the tree line.

On the way to Birk Street, she looked over her shoulder often and watched everyone that passed.

She always knew she couldn't trust anyone. She realized her mistake in trusting Mary with her secret. Trusting her mother was out of the question, or she would have told her what was happening.

Now she had confirmation that a strange man had been watching her at the fair. He had called her at home. That could mean he knew where she lived.

And he wants my notebook, she thought. *Why is everyone so interested in my notebook?*

While walking toward the downtown area, she ran her hands over her forearms, searching for any remaining hair she could pull out.

Chapter 8

Esmerelda stubbed her foot and almost fell, getting into her trailer. She cut herself preparing vegetables. Her forehead still had a small goose egg from when she bumped into a cupboard.

Anxiety made her clumsy. Why was Sarah breaking into the psychic fair's property? Why were Dolan and Alex so interested in her?

After the police had taken Sarah home, Dolan and his assistant questioned Esmerelda for almost an hour. It broached on harassment. Nothing she said had satisfied them. They were convinced she knew more. Dolan said that Sarah had left a message at the admissions desk for her and that that was proof Esmerelda was involved with this young girl somehow.

Esmerelda eased her heavy frame onto the blanket-covered chair in the corner nook of her trailer. She sipped raspberry tea as she tried to decide what to do.

What she didn't tell the others was how Sarah reminded her of her own daughter, Denise. It was uncanny how similar they were in appearance, except for the hair thing. And what was that all about? Did the girl lose it because of some medical condition, or did she pull it out herself? If so, why would she do such a thing?

When Esmerelda saw Sarah yesterday, she thought she was looking at a younger Denise. It broke her heart because she hadn't talked to her daughter since her own husband's death.

John Hall had left everything to their daughter—not a penny was willed to Esmerelda. Her family had not approved of psychic readings, calling it a sin.

Her husband's will was specific. Once John's company was dissolved, a trust fund was set up for Denise. If Esmerelda managed to access any of it, the trust fund would be dispersed to charity.

This callousness had driven Esmerelda out two years before her husband's death. They'd separated, and Esmerelda had joined the psychic fair to travel with Dolan. The only conversation she'd had with Denise about John's death was when her daughter called to ask why she wasn't at the funeral.

That was almost twenty years ago.

When Sarah had walked into the fair yesterday, Esmerelda couldn't help but stare.

Her husband and daughter were a part of the past. Meeting Sarah and seeing a younger Denise in her face was more than a coincidence. It was time for mother and daughter to talk. Something told her she would see her daughter again soon.

Esmerelda grabbed her cell phone and dialed information. Then she stopped, hit end, set the phone down, and leaned back in her chair. Maybe it was too late. She will try to contact Denise tomorrow.

The remote sat on the table to her right. She picked it up and turned the TV on. She flipped through channels until she got to the news. The news anchor pleaded for the girl who pulled her from the river to come forward. A story came on about a kidnapping a few months back and how a teenager had intervened but disappeared before anyone could talk to her. The news story set Esmerelda's thoughts in motion.

Dolan sometimes helped locate missing people. He had worked with the police countless times, even though he hated it. It wasn't that he didn't like helping children—it was the notoriety it gave him that he complained about. The psychic fair would get busier after he was in the paper or on the news for finding a missing child. People would swarm him for help with lost loved ones. They would stay after the fair had closed, trying to get a chance to talk to Dolan.

An odd thought struck her. If Dolan could locate kidnap victims, then why couldn't he just tell the police where the kidnappers themselves were?

Esmerelda leaned forward and set her cup on the table before her shaking hands spilled the tea. Could it be possible that Sarah knew something about this? Maybe that's why Dolan's name was in her book. It would explain all the interest Dolan and Alex had in her.

Esmerelda had to talk to Sarah, and evidently, Sarah had wanted to speak to her.

A thump from the window behind her made her jump.

She spun around in her chair just in time to see the edge of a face disappear.

She got up and went to the kitchen. In her baking supply cabinet, she found a rolling pin. The light switch was near the door. To turn it off would expose her to the open window and whoever may still be out there.

Her hands shook so badly that she almost dropped the rolling pin.

With the light on, she was too visible. She would have to risk being in the open to turn it off.

She leaned across the hallway, flicked off the lights, and dropped down, her back against the door. She sat there, listening for any sounds outside the trailer.

After a few moments of silence, she let her breath wheeze out.

The doorknob rattled. Her free hand covered her mouth as a squeak slipped out.

She looked up at the brass knob as it stopped moving.

Then she edged away from the door with as much stealth as she could muster, picked up her cell, and dialed 911.

Chapter 9

THE CIGARETTE DROPPED INTO the ashtray, where Denise Hall butted it out. She had held it too long. Ashes had fallen from the tip and now lay in her lap. She moved to brush them off, smearing them in the red skirt that covered her thigh.

Documents lay before her on the desk in disarray. Denise gathered them up and tossed them into a corner tray. She picked up her phone and hit speed dial.

When the phone was answered, she wasted no time.

"Any word yet?"

"No, but I'm down at the motel sizing things up."

"Do whatever's necessary. Just tell me if it'll work or not."

"It looks like a fit. I think it'll work. We just need to punch out one wall and set up a secure perimeter. Once the subject is relocated here, we can finish the reconstruction. This means we can move within a day."

"Call me with confirmation."

She rubbed a palm against her throbbing forehead after hanging up. Pausing long enough to control her breathing, she rose from her chair, grabbed her coat, and flicked off the lights. The lock clicked as she turned the key.

An image of her mother briefly entered her head. She stood on the doorstep of her office, eyes closed.

Whatever happened to her? What made me think about my mother?

Maybe it was that stupid psychic stuff she always went on about. Maybe her mother planted a thought in her head from afar.

She laughed. *Craziness.*

Her mother had left for the circus many years ago. At least, that was what her father had called the psychic fair. He used to ridicule her after she left. He would say that it wasn't *Mother knows best* with Esmerelda. It was *Mother knows everything.*

Rain started to hit the pavement. She watched it, remembering she had read last week that rain fell at approximately twenty-seven kilometers an hour.

She lifted her small purse over her head and ran for the car. After getting in, she opened the glovebox and pulled out a small silver flask filled with ten-year-old Scotch. She had beaten alcohol's grip on her months ago but had only recently started again.

The rain sounded like a small machine gun as it pounded the roof. She held still a moment, listening to the rhythm of it. Water seeped down the back of her neck from her wet hair.

Her cell phone chirped. She recapped the flask and tossed it into the glovebox, slamming the little door hard.

Maybe some other time, she thought as she answered the phone.

"Yeah?"

"It'll work. One-hundred percent. Everything measures perfect."

"Good. Send them in. Get it ready for delivery. You know the drill. Do it quietly. I want no one to know you're there. Understood?"

"I'm on it."

She killed the call and tossed the phone on the passenger seat.

She found herself staring at the glovebox. Her mother came to mind again. She wondered if Esmerelda was still alive. Imagine if her mother knew what she had done with the trust fund left to her.

She reached over and opened the glovebox again.

Chapter 10

PEOPLE NORMALLY STARED AT her face or looked away fast because of the lack of hair. For the past hour, as she walked toward her appointment with another kidnapping, she had not noticed anyone paying extra attention to her. Her shirt sleeves dropped below the elbow. Her bandanna was a red one tonight, the one she usually wore to do her notebook's bidding.

Sarah watched the passersby more than they watched her. The danger Esmerelda had talked about was out there, but she also felt a sense of foreboding as if, somehow, *she* was being watched.

Maybe it was the call in her father's den that was spooking her?

To top it all off, Mary couldn't be trusted either. An earlier precognition had told her to use Mary, so she did. But she hadn't been comfortable with it.

She was a few blocks from downtown, about a thirty-minute walk to Birk Street. She passed by a storefront and stopped. She needed to know the time, but she'd left her watch at home in her hurry to leave. She pried the crumpled piece of paper out of her pocket and opened it to the message.

Tonight. 9:23 p.m. Birk Street. North Face. Kidnapping.

She slipped the paper into a large pocket below the knee area of her cargo pants. She almost wished she could just call the police and tell them what would happen, let them handle it. That was their job, anyway. She knew the answer to that, though. She hated cops. Ever since the cop who used to babysit her years ago as a favor to her mother had done things to her, she despised every single officer on the planet. She shivered at the memory. She would never be able to trust a cop. Ever.

Thinking about the past only made her want to pull. She stepped into the store she'd been standing in front of, checked the clock on the wall, and stepped back out to the sidewalk.

8:30 p.m.

She pushed the red bandanna a little above her ear. Stray hairs tumbled out. Savoring the moment as she continued toward Birk Street, she took her time easing them from their roots. She could almost feel the exact moment when the follicles disengaged.

She dropped her hand and stuffed it into her pants pocket. The hairs she'd claimed from her scalp were entwined through her fingers. She rolled them around, trying to quell her nervousness.

Neither did she want this, nor did she ask for it. She didn't like the police in her life, either. Sitting in the back of their cruiser earlier had been horrible. It made her feel weak.

She was weak once. Filled with despair, loneliness, depression.

After the incident with the babysitter, she remembered how she had withdrawn. He had told her that his fellow officers watched over him. They would be watching her, too. If a cop ever took a statement about what happened between them, they would throw it in the garbage after she was out of sight. He even nodded and waved to a fellow officer in her presence.

Sarah shook her head. Memories of those days always rattled her. This wasn't the best time for that, but they were like a memory tumor, always eating away at her on the inside.

She came to a busy intersection, crossed on the green, and continued south.

There were a couple of dark years after that when her depression went unnoticed by her parents. They only got juiced about the decline in her school report cards.

And now, her entire eyebrows and lashes were gone. Most of her forearm hair was missing, along with small amounts of pubic hair. The bandanna on her head covered what hair she had left.

Her mother had taken her to the doctor to discover why Sarah lost so much hair, and they had misdiagnosed it as *Alopecia areata*. Sarah never let on that she had anything to do with the missing hair. At the time, they thought it was a fungal infection. A few years later, as Sarah's *condition* failed to see results from medication, her mother took her to see a new doctor. This doctor diagnosed her with *trichotillomania*. Some people were cutters, using razor blades as a form of self-mutilation to calm their anxieties. Sarah was a puller.

The doctor prescribed Zoloft, which she refused to take because she enjoyed being alone, depressed. She didn't want to be like everyone else, happy and fake. The dark moods were something she didn't want to discard. They had become a companion, a form of comfort.

Besides, it wasn't like she wanted a lot of friends. She couldn't do some of the basic things friends did together, like swimming in a public pool. Everyone would notice the hair loss, and she wouldn't fit in.

Sarah had never fit in.

In the beginning, she tried to only pull from the regions of her body that were less noticeable, staying away from her head. As hair thinned, it became harder to find quality strands. Then her head was fair game, starting above the nape of her neck where it wouldn't be seen as much, spreading from there.

Would her parents notice her if she pulled all her hair out then? Would they stop arguing about her?

Sarah slowed up about a block and a half from Birk Street. She had to collect herself, get her thoughts back to the job at hand. She wiped a tear away and took a couple of deep breaths.

After a moment, she started walking again. What did *North Face* mean? Was the victim going to face north or be on the north side of the street? Then she recalled Birk Street ran east and west. It was a relatively short street, intersecting with the entertainment district.

Within minutes she had walked up to the corner of Birk and Acton Street. A theater on Birk was showing the new movie with Brad Pitt. To the left, she saw a convenience store and a Topper's Pizza. People were milling around the pizza shop, waiting for the late show.

Maybe *North Face* was meant for *her* to face north. She looked up and down Birk Street. How was she supposed to know who would be kidnapped and who would do the kidnapping, especially with all these people hanging around?

This precognition seemed to have more unknowns than the others. They were never too clear, but at least in other messages, she was given an article of clothing, a hair color, or something specific to watch for or do, like *Bring Hammer*.

Not this time.

She turned to her right and walked down about half a block. A clock on the inside wall of a closed barber shop said 9:10 p.m.

The barbershop's door sat recessed, hidden from the street. Sarah stepped up, turned, and leaned against it. From her vantage point, she could almost see the whole north side of Birk Street, including the entrance to the theater and the pizza joint where most of the people converged. She could even smell the pizzas cooking from where she stood.

While she waited, she reread the note.

I'm as prepared as I can be, she thought, trying to quell her stomach.

After Esmerelda warned about danger, she wondered what she was doing here. If what she was about to do *was* the danger, she could be in a lot of trouble. The police should be the ones watching this street. She may not like or trust them, but not all cops are bad. They could have the street surrounded at this very moment if she had told them what would happen. She would have had more credibility if she had revealed who she really was. The news anchorwoman would broadcast her as a hero, and the other people she saved would verify her story. It truly seemed irrational for her not to involve the police.

Nevertheless, she could not bring herself to put any trust in law enforcement. And she did not want to be a public person, made out to be some hero across the media.

She glanced in the barbershop window.

9:20 p.m.

In three minutes, someone will be kidnapped on this street.

Not only did Sarah not know *who*, but she also did not know *where* exactly.

Chapter 11

GERT SAT IN THE passenger seat, wondering why his brother was being such a dick. They had been staking out the theater for an hour, waiting for their intended victim to show up.

He had done all the hard work on this one—scouting the place out, following the girl. He almost got caught watching her house. Gert always obeyed commands because he respected his older brother. If it hadn't been for Matt, he wouldn't be doing this at all. He would probably be in jail by now.

Matt was the one who handled the boss. Matt was the one barking the orders, and he was the one who always got paid more money.

Enough was enough. Gert wanted a little something. He wanted to play around a little with the next girl they took. He didn't care how old she was. If she was old enough to bleed, she was old enough to breed.

"So, how about it?" Gert pleaded with his brother. "Why not?"

"No way. You know what the boss thinks of that stuff. Personally, I think the boss would have you taken out if you were too rough with any of the subjects."

"Where's the fun in just kidnapping them? Why can't we have a little something on the side?"

"I'll tell ya what. The next time I talk to the boss, I'll hand you the phone. You can ask him yourself."

Gert shook his hands back and forth, waving that notion off. "Forget it. That's like asking permission to get laid. No way. Not me. I don't ask permission for that."

"Since you're asking me then, I think there might be a reason you want permission. Could it be you're afraid of the additional criminal charges if you're ever caught?"

"You mean arrested?"

"Yeah, dummy. They can only charge you with kidnapping if you never touch the girls. You fuck one of them, and now, not only do they get you on kidnapping, but they'll have you on a whole slew of sex-related charges. The kind that makes you do serious time. And while you're doing time, someone claims you as his bitch and rips *you* a new one for touching a little girl."

Gert looked at the dash clock and saw it was 9:21 p.m. It was time to talk about something else because he didn't like where this was going. "Once we take the girl, is the place ready for us?"

"Yes. I talked to the boss earlier, and it looks like it's all set up or getting set up. Something like that. Either way, we got the go-ahead to move the girl there after we grab her."

Gert looked down at the floorboards. One of these days, he was going to do his own thing. There was no reason why he couldn't kidnap a stupid rich teenager on his own, set up the money arrangement, and keep every penny for himself. He was practically doing all of it on his own anyway. He could even have his way with the girl for a week or two while she was tied up in a basement or locked in a cage.

Matt smacked his arm and put the car in gear.

"This is it. I'll handle the girl. You keep the boyfriend off our back. Let's do this and be quick about it."

"I still want to fuck her."

Chapter 12

THE MOVIE HAD ENDED, and the people leaving the theater swelled onto the street. The area was getting busy—dozens of people milling around, waiting to get in for the late show.

A girl wearing a blue vest with her date hanging off her shoulder walked right by Sarah. The girl looked up and locked eyes with her. Sarah stared as the couple turned toward the street and walked across to the north side.

There was something about the girl that bothered Sarah. The vest was too warm for a night like this. The streetlights gave off enough light to see the logo on her vest but not the name. It consisted of two edges that looked like an L, with each tip of the L connected by a half circle. It was a familiar brand, but Sarah couldn't put her finger on the name.

She stepped back into the recessed doorway, darkness covering her.

A black Chrysler pulled away from the curb half a block down and started a slow advance toward the pizza joint.

The North Face. She snapped her fingers. That was the company's name with the logo on the girl's vest. *The North Face.*

So she *did* get an identifier for the intended victim, and she had missed it. The girl had been right beside her not one minute ago, and now she was across the street in front of the pizza shop.

Sarah stepped out from the recessed doorway. She had to get to the other side of Birk Street. She had to warn the girl to take cover, get away, hide.

Without looking at another clock, Sarah was pretty sure it was 9:23 p.m.

She stepped onto the street and went to cross, wary of who the kidnappers would be.

Her heart skipped and pounded an extra beat like it was struggling to break a rib. She caught her breath when she looked into the windshield of the Chrysler moving her way. Both men were staring at the *North Face* girl as they eased along.

What shocked her was the man sitting in the car's passenger seat.

She recognized him.

It was the same guy from six months ago—the one who tried to kidnap Mary Bennett. That night, Mary turned and ran back to her dad's car after Sarah pleaded with her to do so. This guy had been in a van that night, the side door open, ready to pull Mary in as the van trolled by. Sarah remembered how he had grabbed at her for interfering. Her bandanna got ripped off her head, and then the man reeled back at the sight of her missing hair. That was the only reason she escaped his grasp.

It was one of her most dangerous exploits to date. She would never forget his face. It had been her first and almost her last.

They hadn't spotted her yet. She could leave. She still had time to get away. *But what about the girl?* Sarah wrestled with the idea of running because of Esmerelda's warning of danger. But could she live with herself if she didn't *try* to stop this?

She put one foot in front of the other and started across the road. Time stood still. The night air touched her, cooling her skin.

Indecision wasn't an option. She could not allow it to be.

The two men had pulled to a stop by the sidewalk fifteen feet from the girl and her boyfriend.

Sarah felt her call to duty. Somehow, she had been chosen. She was being given these messages for a reason. She had no idea what the reason was. What she did know was that she could do something about it.

She made it to the other side of Birk just as the two men came out of their car. They had parked by the curb. The engine was still on. Sarah assumed this was to get out of the area fast.

She looked back at the intended victim. The girl was too far away from her.

The kidnappers would get there first.

She couldn't run and draw attention to herself. She was lost. It was over. What could she do now?

She had failed.

She kept walking anyway, staying close to the wall of the building she was passing. She had to think of something. All hope wasn't lost as long as she was there, and the girl hadn't been taken.

Both men reached into their inner suit jacket pockets in unison. It looked rehearsed. Everything seemed to slow down. The timing was perfect. The girl and her boyfriend had stepped away from a small crowd and were standing in front of the theater doors for a moment. Sarah was close enough to hear the two men from the Chrysler say they were police officers.

She could see both men were showing badges of some sort.

At this point, there was nothing she could do to help the girl get away.

Instead, she decided to get rid of their car.

While the men were busy, she turned and headed toward their idling vehicle. Maybe the best thing would be to snatch the car keys.

She looked down at her shaking legs. They felt weak as the surge of adrenaline faded.

She glanced sideways when she was halfway across the street.

The man she had recognized six months ago looked right at her.

Their eyes locked.

Her feet faltered.

Oh, shit. Okay, run, grab the keys.

Before she turned away, she saw him slap his partner's arm. Both men watched her now.

She bolted. One look over her shoulder told her everything she needed to know. She would never get to the car, reach in, pull the keys out, and escape in time. No way. They would be on her before she got her hands on the keys.

She was still a dozen feet from the car. Footsteps pounded hard and fast behind her. They sounded close. Even if she ran up the street, they'd still catch her. She didn't waste any energy looking behind her again.

The only thing left was the car.

She had to take the car.

In the second it took her to think about it, she was diving into the front seat. She grabbed the driver's side door and pulled hard. Her pursuer stuck his hand in to keep the door open. His fingers yanked out at the last second before Sarah closed and locked it.

Huge gulps of air came from her mouth. The man she recognized from the attempted kidnapping of Mary banged on the door's side window with one hand. She looked up at him. His other hand was pulling keys out of his pocket.

Spare keys with a key fob.

Sarah grabbed the gear shifter beside her leg and tried to push the car into drive.

It wouldn't move. Then her index finger felt a button on the underside of the stick. She put her foot on the brake, depressed the button, and dropped the car into drive.

The doors clicked and unlocked.

She didn't know when she started to scream. It was just coming out of her mouth.

Everything was going wrong.

The driver's side door was pulled away from her.

He was in.

She stomped on the accelerator, lurching the car forward. The man tried to climb into the vehicle but was knocked off his feet. He held onto the car door, being dragged along.

Sarah looked through the windshield and saw the man's partner standing in front of the car.

"Stop, you bitch," the man being dragged screamed.

He reached up, found a small batch of hair sticking out from under the bandanna Sarah wore, and ripped it out. She would have normally laughed at the idea of someone helping her along with what she had started years ago, but that many hairs at once—pulled by someone else—stung like a bitch. Her eyes watered and her vision muddied from the tears.

The sudden pain from the loss of hair caused her to wince and reach a hand back to the injury in reflex. The man let go of the door and rolled away from the car.

She tried to gain control of the vehicle again, but with the driver's side door open and the pain rushing through her, she swerved as she overcorrected the steering wheel. She saw the corner of the car clip the other man standing out front.

His head bounced against the hood like a basketball. Then he disappeared from Sarah's view. She hit the brake and stopped the car.

She couldn't quell the shaking. A part of her reasoned she would be safe now. No one would try to hurt her with all these witnesses.

She could feel something dripping on her shoulder. She touched where the hair had been ripped from her head. She looked down at her hand to see it was covered in blood.

The guy she had recognized walked past the open driver's side door. His interest in her had died off for the moment. His face was a mask of shock.

Sarah eased herself out of the car. People had stopped their vehicles. Pedestrians were coming off the sidewalks to get a closer look. Someone yelled for someone else to call an ambulance.

Sarah came around to the front of the car, holding her head where her hair had come out. Tears blurred her vision.

The man she'd hit lay on the ground. His eyes were open wide. As far as Sarah could tell, he was dead.

She had killed him. Her stomach rebelled. She felt faint.

A man was now dead because of her actions.

She doubled over, nausea coursing through her.

A dead man. She was supposed to help people, not kill them.

She had done it.

From the corner of her eye, she saw someone materialize next to her. She turned to look at him.

He was holding a gun. Someone in the crowd behind her gasped.

"Who *are* you?" the man asked.

Sarah couldn't answer. She wondered if her legs could hold her weight any longer. She leaned on the car.

"Where did you come from? Why did you show up again? Who the *fuck* are you?" He was shouting now.

He walked around his partner's body, knelt, and felt for a pulse, keeping his gun trained on Sarah the whole time.

"Whoever you are, you will die for killing my brother. You just made Heaven's most wanted list." He stepped closer. "I wonder what you would look like with half your *face* missing."

His eyes were wide, swishing back and forth in their sockets.

"My gun is loaded with hollowed-out bullets, which causes the exit wound to be a gaping hole. It leaves a small entry in your cheek, half your brains on the street. So get moving, or you'll have a personal meeting with one of my many hollowed-out friends. Get in the car now before these crowds get bigger."

Sarah couldn't move. Her feet felt rooted to the ground. She wondered if this was what it felt like when shock set in.

The gun was a foot from her face. It moved a little to the right and discharged. The loud report made her jump and blink. The *whoosh* where the air was torn to allow the bullet passage rang in her ear. She could faintly hear people screaming. Someone ran past her so close they bumped her arm.

The world had gone crazy, chaotic.

"I won't waste another bullet," the madman shouted. "Talk to God about it, or get in the car."

Sarah tried to move but still felt too weak.

Then darkness set in, and she fell to the ground in a heap.

Chapter 13

Esmerelda scrunched down against the kitchen cupboards while she waited for the police to arrive, rolling pin in hand. After ten minutes, she could hear people talking outside. It sounded like the security guard, which meant the police had shown up.

She opened her trailer door to see two officers talking with the guard. She met with them and relayed what had happened. Both officers walked around her trailer, inspecting it for signs of attempted entry or damage. After finding nothing amiss, they told her they would swing by hourly for the rest of the night and reminded her that she was in a gated area guarded by security personnel. She reminded them of how easy it was for someone to breach security, as proved by the earlier incident.

An hour passed. The police had come and gone. Esmerelda fixed another cup of tea and checked the windows to ensure all the curtains were pulled shut. She took a sip from her mug and wondered if she should call Sarah now or tomorrow. No doubt she would have gotten into trouble with her parents when she arrived home in a police cruiser.

Esmerelda wanted to explain the incident to Sarah's parents as a misunderstanding. She would tell them it was a case of overzealous security or something to that effect.

She also wanted to talk to Sarah to find out why she had been so persistent in contacting her earlier.

She picked up the note with Sarah's phone number, given to her by Dolan, who had grabbed it from the cashiers at the front and dialed. On the third ring, it was answered.

"Hello?"

"Could I speak to Sarah, please?" Esmerelda hoped her voice didn't betray her nervousness following the evening's police visit and the attempted break-in.

"Who's this?" demanded the female voice on the other end of the line. Esmerelda assumed it was Sarah's mother.

"My name is Esmerelda. I saw you yesterday at the psychic fair when you came to pick up your daughter."

"Esmerelda? Why do you people keep calling for Sarah? I don't want to be rude here, but this is the second call in one day."

"Someone else called looking for Sarah?" Esmerelda asked.

"Yes. A man. As soon as he called, Sarah ran out of the house."

"Did he give a name?"

"No. He said he wanted to talk to Sarah and that he was from the fair."

"Would you be able to describe his voice for me?"

"What's this all about? Why all the sudden interest in my daughter?" Sarah's mother sounded anxious and scared.

Esmerelda switched the phone to her other ear. "I'm as puzzled as you are. I've been a member of the psychic fair for many years. I would know anyone's voice over the phone if they were an actual representative of the fair."

"Well, I have no idea how to describe a voice to you. All I can say is that it was a man." She paused. "Wait a minute. Are you suggesting someone else called for my daughter and only *said* they were from the fair?"

Esmerelda cleared her throat. Raspberry scents drifted from her mug beside her. She took a deep breath and tried to relax.

"I'm talking to her mother, right?" Esmerelda asked. "You're the one I saw at the fair."

"Yes. My name is Amelia, and my husband is Caleb."

Time for some honesty.

"Amelia, I think Sarah may be in trouble."

"Trouble?"

"How long has she been gone?"

"All afternoon and evening, why?"

"I think it best if you call the police and go on record that you want to report your daughter as a missing person."

Esmerelda heard an audible gasp over the line.

"What're you talking about?" Amelia's voice was almost a shriek now. "What information do you have to say such a thing?"

Through the receiver, Esmerelda could hear something scrape on a tile floor. It sounded like Sarah's mother took a seat on a kitchen chair.

"Because you're telling me this," Amelia continued, "it means you know something. What do you know about my daughter?"

"When I met Sarah, I saw her gift and its drawbacks."

"Gift? Drawbacks? None of this makes sense. Are you talking about the news lady in the river? Do you know what's happening to my daughter?"

"All I know is she's probably in trouble. I tried to warn her yesterday."

"Okay. Since you won't tell me what you know specifically, I will call the police, and they'll pay you a visit. Maybe you'll tell them what you know. You have to understand how crazy this sounds. Yesterday Sarah went to the psychic fair, today, my daughter comes home in a police car accused of breaking into the fair, and then we get two phone calls from the fair looking for her. The first sends her out the door; the second tells me she's in trouble …"

"I know how this must look, but I don't know more because my ability isn't absolute. I can't just ask questions and get answers. Psychic ability is more of a feeling, an intuition."

"You're kidding. I saw you yesterday. You're just like the rest of the false prophets, and now you're calling to tell me my daughter is missing. What's really going on? Tell me what you know."

"Ma'am, I'm not involved in any way. I merely tried …"

"I'm calling the police. Goodbye, Esmerelda."

The line went dead. Esmerelda replaced the phone and stood. She had thought she could help, but she had only done more harm. She entered her kitchen and got another pot of tea brewing. It was going to be a long night, indeed. She expected another visit from the police after that phone call.

She picked up the remote and turned on her little 20-inch TV. The news covered a hit-and-run in front of a pizza place on Birk Street that had just happened. Television crews were on site, and witnesses were being paraded in front of the cameras.

A young man, about seventeen years old, said he had seen a Chrysler hit and kill a man—a car driven by a young woman wearing a red bandanna. He stated that another man had grabbed the girl, put her in the car, and sped off.

Another teenager said she would recognize that face anywhere. She knew the girl in the red bandanna. They had gone to the same high school.

She was definitely Sarah Roberts.

The news capped the story by saying that the police were now looking for eighteen-year-old Sarah Roberts for questioning in the hit-and-run murder of an as-yet-unidentified male Caucasian.

Chapter 14

Amelia heard her husband entering the house.

The magic they had once shared died years ago with their firstborn, Vivian.

Not a day went by that Amelia didn't think of her. Sometimes she wondered if Caleb did.

Their relationship had become routine. They were like roommates who had committed to each other to stick it out until their other daughter grew up and moved on.

She sat in the living room, trying to work on a piece of pie.

"You're home late." She put her fork down and looked up at him. "We need to talk." She didn't wait for a response. "Sarah's missing."

Caleb had removed his overcoat and was sorting through a pile of mail on the small stand by the front door. He acted as if he hadn't heard her.

"What do you mean, *missing*?"

"She left the house and hasn't returned. It's not like her to come home after midnight."

Amelia picked up her fork and ran it over the top of the pie, fiddling with the crust.

"That doesn't qualify as missing. Is there something else?" Caleb walked over and stood in front of the coffee table.

"I got a call from that psychic woman Sarah talked about yesterday. Apparently, she warned Sarah about some kind of trouble she would be in."

Caleb dropped the envelopes on the coffee table. He turned and planted himself in the La-Z-Boy opposite the couch. "What psychic woman? From the fair?"

"The one from yesterday who Sarah said gave her a reading."

"You've got to be kidding," Caleb said and looked up at the ceiling. "If this was real, and she knew about the danger, why just vaguely warn us? Why not tell us when and where so we could prevent it?" He raised his hands in the air. "You know why? Because there are no psychics. It's all a crock. If this psychic woman said Sarah was in danger, and *then* something happened to Sarah, it's either a coincidence or that *psychic* woman is involved somehow."

"She advised me to call the police."

Caleb put his hands on either side of his head and gripped his hair in frustration. "She called here? How did she get our number?"

Amelia ignored the question. "That's not all. A man called just before Sarah left. He said he was from the fair, too. He didn't give a name."

"What's going on? I knew that fair was a mistake from the beginning." Caleb shook his head.

Amelia got up from the couch and dropped her plate on the mail. She turned and faced Caleb.

"Sarah tried to break into the psychic fairgrounds today. Security caught her and sent her home with the police. They gave her a stern warning."

Caleb put his hand up for her to stop. "She just went to the fair yesterday. We picked her up. Why would she *break in*? Amelia, tell me you're joking. I've already lost one daughter. I'm not about to lose another. Are we in trouble here?"

"Correction. *We've* lost one daughter."

"You know what I mean."

"No, I don't. Tell me what you mean, Caleb." Amelia raised her voice. "That has always bothered me. I know you blame me for losing Vivian that day. You feel I was less of a mother. You refer to Vivian as if she was only your daughter. She was mine too," Amelia said. She touched her chest with her hand.

Caleb dropped his head. "I'm sorry. You're right. We all grieve in our own way. It's a very personal thing for me." He fiddled with a fingernail. "When I think of her, I think about her as my little girl. With no pictures on the walls, since we decided not to tell Sarah about her sister until she was older, my only memories are in my head. Over the years, those memories grew to something so personal that they became my memories alone." He folded his hands behind his head. "I never meant to exclude you, but we can't even talk about Vivian out loud because we have to keep it from Sarah. Which, by the way, I don't agree with anymore."

Amelia stepped away from the couch, moving behind it. She crossed her arms. "I don't want to tell Sarah yet. She's got enough problems with that notebook and her hair pulling. We only recently started helping her out of her depression. I think we should wait a couple of years. I know she's eighteen, but she acts fourteen."

"If we keep waiting, there may be a point where we shouldn't tell her. She'll wonder if she could trust us after keeping such a secret for so long. I'm beginning to wonder if we made the right choice in the first place. We could've told her about her sister, just not how she was killed. And now Sarah isn't home at this late hour, and we're panicking. This is insane. I can't lose two daughters."

Amelia used the back of her hand to wipe a tear away. "There you go again. *I can't lose two daughters* like you're the only parent."

Caleb raised his eyes to look at her but kept his face pointing downward. "We've gone over this. We need to figure out what's going on with Sarah. I think we argued enough last night about letting her go to that stupid fair in the first place. Now look at the problems we've got."

Amelia walked back around and sat down on the couch. "Okay, so should we call the police?"

Caleb frowned, unclasped his hands, and rubbed his chin. "Since she has only been gone a few hours—"

He was interrupted by a familiar beeping from his suit jacket by the front door. Amelia watched as he grabbed his coat and pulled his cell phone from the inside pocket.

"I wonder who would text me at this hour?" he said.

He clicked a few buttons and then read out loud. "Hi, Dad, it's Sarah. I thought I'd let you know that I'm staying at Mary's house tonight. Don't worry. Mom knows who she is. See you in the morning. Love Sarah." Caleb stopped reading and looked up. "Who's Mary?"

"We talked on the phone earlier today. She called before Sarah arrived home in a police car."

"What did she want?"

"She told me some interesting things. She said Sarah writes prophecies in her notebook. Then she goes out and saves people. Apparently, Mary is someone Sarah saved from being kidnapped six months ago."

"Impossible. We can't be this far out of the loop. That's ridiculous. Are you talking about our Sarah?"

Amelia nodded. "Come to think of it, Sarah said she was going to meet Mary or something like that when she ran out."

"This is unbelievable. Did you ask Sarah about what Mary said? Where's her notebook?"

"Sarah said she lost the notebook. The phone rang when we were in her bedroom looking for it. It was the guy from the fair. Right after that, she left."

"Do you have Mary's phone number?"

"I think so. It should be on call display."

"I'll call her. We'll straighten this out right now."

Chapter 15

SARAH WOKE TO DARKNESS. She realized she was in the trunk of a car, her confined space bumping and moving with the subtle susurrations of the vehicle. A soft red glow showed her where the taillights were.

She tried to move her hands but realized they were tied behind her back. Her wrists were alarmingly numb when she didn't move them and shrieked with pain when she did. Her head pounded where the hair had been pulled out.

She tried to swish her feet back and forth, but her ankles were bound and numb, too. When her head moved, the dried and crusty blood on the back of her neck tightened.

She opened her mouth to scream.

Stupid asshole, she thought. *He didn't gag me.*

"Help!" she yelled, knowing her plea would not be heard too well outside the trunk of a moving car. Her lungs starved for air. Panting and gasping, she struggled harder and tried to scream again. Nothing much higher than a nasal screech came out.

Rapid breaths from her nose were not enough to sate her lungs. A lightheaded feeling of suffocation made her set her head down and slow her breathing.

What did I get myself into?

She was tied up in a trunk, a victim of a kidnapper, or worse. And she had just killed someone.

Deeper, slower breathing kept her awake. She had to stay alert.

The car hit a bump in the road. Her shoulder flared up in pain, making her wince.

She wished she could pull. Find some hair in a sensitive spot and drag it out slowly. That would help to calm her down. She needed to get untied so she could pull.

The engine started to wind down. Either the driver was approaching a traffic light or stopping the car.

A bead of sweat rolled into her eye. She clenched her eyelid closed and shook her head. The headache flared. Nothing was working. Nothing was going her way.

Gravel crunched under the tires moments before the car stopped. She struggled to hold her breath so she could listen to the sounds from the outside.

The car door opened, and she felt the weight adjust as the driver got out. Her heart beat a rhythm in her ear canal.

The trunk lid popped open. It remained an inch above the lock until fingers slid through the crack and lifted it.

She didn't know what to expect. Would he shoot her in the trunk? Is there a deep pond or a batch of trees nearby where her body could rot for years undetected?

What she didn't expect was the flashlight. The man flicked one on, instantly blinding her.

"Never try to scream from the trunk again. There are painful ways to die. You don't want that, trust me." The man's voice was filled with pure hatred.

He lashed out hard and fast. Lightning flared in her vision when she was hit with something like a brick. The pain was almost unbearable. Her face was aflame now. She couldn't help the scream that came out. The other side of her face had slammed into the bottom of the trunk in response to the force of the blow.

A coppery taste filled her mouth. She opened her eyes. They still worked. Things would look different if an eye socket or cheekbone were broken.

"Rules," he said. "That's one thing my brother taught me. Follow the rules."

His rough hands grabbed her shirt and lifted her. Bound behind her, her arms and legs screamed in protest. She couldn't suppress her moaning.

His face was inches from hers now.

"I've broken a few rules for you already today. You weren't the intended target. So I expect you to follow the rules I set. Rule number one: no screaming. The next time you scream for anybody, I'll teach you what screaming really is."

He shoved her backward. Her head smacked the back of the open trunk lid right where he had removed the clump of hair earlier. She landed awkwardly on her arms, twisting her left elbow. By the time she could think to right herself, the trunk lid was shut, closing her into darkness again.

With the pain coursing through every nerve in her body, an odd thought struck her, *what was rule number two?*

She could hear a cell phone ringing. She closed her eyes and focused on her breathing. Through the thin metal of the trunk, she heard him answer it.

"Hello?"

She waited, straining to hear more.

"Matt's dead … I know, but I got that girl from six months ago … I have no idea why she was there … this is so fucked up … what am I going to do without Matt? I've never done this alone."

She heard his voice decrease in volume. He moved out of earshot.

"That's just it … where do you want me to dump her body?"

Then he was too far away to hear anymore.

She curled into a ball and couldn't stop the tears. Mary would've texted her dad by now. No one knew where she was, and no one would start looking for her until tomorrow or even the day after. She was on her own.

The car door slammed shut moments later, and they were moving again.

Sarah wept in the darkness until she fell asleep.

Before she lost consciousness, Sarah realized she had identified the danger Esmerelda had warned her about.

Chapter 16

DENISE HALL ORDERED A glass of brandy. She wanted her nerves calmed for the meeting. She sat at the bar of an American version of a pub. This one reeked like it hadn't been cleaned in months.

She thought about all the deals she had done in the past. This would be her biggest sale to her richest and most notorious client.

She pushed her sleeve aside and read the time. The pub would be closing soon. She was thirty minutes early for the meeting.

Good.

You did not want to be late for Mr. Ward. Anyone who was anyone knew that.

Her stomach lurched uneasily at the smell of greasy food. Something unidentifiable was burning in the back. She took a long swig of her drink.

The front door opened, and two large men dressed in suits and matching crew cuts entered the pub. They looked around until both pairs of eyes stopped on Denise. Then they continued scanning the small pub, taking it all in.

A waitress approached them only to be waved off.

Denise took another long sip and watched the men who had taken a position on either side of the door. It looked rather odd—two sentries guarding the inside of a restaurant.

She smirked at the thought of how nervous she was. She had dealt with Mr. Ward on several other arrangements in the past. Why would this sale be any different? She also understood the routine. If she wanted to sell to him, she had to play along.

She didn't have to *like* it. She just had to play along.

He was the kind of man the mafia respected.

Maybe I'm being too kind, she thought.

He was short, no more than five feet tall, with a large net worth—the kind that required better security than the president.

Sometimes Denise wondered about the ethics of what she was doing. And sometimes she wondered about people in India. Who cared about everyone else? Look out for number one, and in the end, you die. There was nothing else to worry about. Maybe that was why she no longer talked to her mother.

She took another drink from her glass as one of the men at the door responded to his cell phone. He put it away and nodded to the other. They broke from sentry duty and walked to Denise's table.

"Come with us," the taller one grunted.

It was always the same.

"Let me finish my drink."

"Now. Stand."

Again, just like before. She wouldn't let them take her dignity. It was only a business transaction. She put the glass to her lips.

One of the men reached under her arm, half lifting her to her feet. She was almost carried to the door and taken outside to the cool early July morning, her drink glass still in her hand.

Mr. Ward's car was not there. No surprise. The trio turned right and then into an alleyway. Another larger man stood in front of the back door of what looked like a Chinese restaurant. They guided her down a dark set of stairs.

So Hollywood, she thought wryly.

They entered a dank basement. Single bulbs hung with strings attached. Either the walls were painted black and decaying after years of moisture, or they were covered in mold. It was too dim to see, for sure.

Mr. Ward sat behind a table near the far wall. He sat alone, watching her approach. This would be quite intimidating if she didn't deal with him before. It certainly was the first time she had met him.

"Sit," he said, gesturing with his hand to the wooden grade-school chair in front of the table.

The apes on each side of her fell away, and she once again had full use of her feet. She set the brandy glass on the table.

"Do you have the package?" Mr. Ward asked.

He was one of those men who always talked with a smile like he was the only one who knew the inside joke.

"I got confirmation earlier. That's why I called to meet you."

He stared at her through sunglasses so dark she couldn't see his eyes.

Denise knew the tough guy thing was all an act. He had to make sure his employees never forgot who the boss was.

"How am I to expect delivery?"

"I have a discreet location renovated to keep your package safe. The renovations will be completed today, and the package will arrive tomorrow. I'll call then and set up the arrangements."

"The money will be wired to your usual account. When you call with the package location, and I confirm possession of the package, the money will transfer, as usual."

Denise nodded. It was always the same routine. The meeting was only a formality. She stood to leave.

"May I go now?" she asked.

Mr. Ward nodded.

This time, unaided by the gorillas, she walked toward the stairs. When she reached them, she looked back at Mr. Ward. He hadn't moved an inch.

"I wanted to say that this package is different. It has caused me a lot of trouble. This one is a real piece of work. I hope you're going to be happy with it."

"My emotions aren't your concern," Mr. Ward said with his trademark smile.

Denise headed up the stairs, trailing the smell of chicken fried rice, her stomach in knots.

Chapter 17

THE SOUND AND RHYTHM of the car had a soothing quality. Every breath she took, every second that went by, was another second she was alive. Also, every second that went by, she desperately had to pee, but she tried hard to ignore it.

The driver recognized her from Mary's kidnapping, which she suspected was why she wasn't dead yet. He would want to find out why she had shown up twice.

He would probably try to extract this information through violence, she thought with a shudder.

The engine's noise changed, and she felt the brakes being applied. The car turned onto a gravel road—her bladder was about to burst. Rocks careened off the wheel well by her head. The car turned again and then came to a stop. Then silence.

She had no idea where they were. He could very well open the trunk, pull her out, shoot her in the face, and throw her body behind a tree. She squeezed her eyes shut. *Can't keep thinking like that*, she scolded herself. *Stay positive.*

The trunk lid sprang open. She opened her eyes. It was dark outside. There was a single light as high as one found on any city street.

He yanked her from the trunk and let go. She dropped to the gravel. The sting was intense. Her arms and legs felt rubbery. She just wanted to lie there and rest with a morphine drip attached to her arm.

She saw the glint of a blade in the light. Before she realized it was a knife, its downward arc came swiftly.

Her ankles fell apart. She twisted her head away as he came toward her face. She felt a slight tug, and then her hands dropped apart.

The driver stepped back and then turned and walked away. She followed his footsteps with her gaze. He got to the front of a cabin, fidgeted with the door, and opened it. He flicked a light on inside the building and turned to face her from the porch.

"If you're thinking about running, there's no place to go. Scream if you like. We're miles away from civilization. No one will hear you. I wouldn't scream, though. That would defy rule number one."

He seemed to be enjoying himself. Something had changed in his demeanor. He grinned wide, his smile a beacon of insanity.

"You should make yourself comfortable while you still can. There isn't much time for you left."

If he wanted to kill her, he would have done it. Keeping a hostage required much more work and added an element of risk.

"I'll give you one minute to get in here," he said, disappearing inside the cabin.

Trees surrounded the area. She eyed the road they had come in on. It turned away from her and was lost in darkness. In the distance, what sounded like transport trucks raced along a highway.

She looked back at the cabin. He was watching her from a window to the right of the door.

She tried to get to her feet. They worked, but with pins and needles. She stood using the back of the car for support. The effort caused pain to flare up in her face where he had hit her.

She could not outrun him. He was still watching her, his deadline of one minute looming. No point in testing him too early.

She started across the gravel for the cabin door. How could the precognition be so wrong? Why was she here?

She was eighteen and now a full-grown woman, but she felt small and needy.

After all the people she had saved, who was coming for her?

Chapter 18

"I CAN'T GET AN answer. No one's picking up the phone," Amelia said as she replaced the receiver. "It's been an hour since we got the text."

Caleb grabbed his cell phone and started pressing buttons.

"What're you doing?" Amelia asked.

"Why didn't I think of it before? I don't know how I missed it. When we sent those replies to the phone where the text came from, asking them to call us, I forgot that it was another cell phone. Whoever sent us that message used a cell that I can call." Caleb's thumb worked the tiny keys. "There, got it."

Amelia watched him as he lifted the phone to his ear. He looked at her and shook his head back and forth.

"Machine." He dropped the phone from his head. "Dead end."

"Well, what do we do now?" Amelia asked. She rubbed her hands together as if she was putting lotion on them. "I can't sit around. Sarah isn't home, and it's past midnight." She grabbed the phone again. "I'm calling the police."

Caleb didn't try to stop her.

The phone rang in her hand. She jumped and swung around to look at Caleb. He motioned for her to answer it. She shook her head and handed the phone to him.

"Hello?" Caleb said.

"My name is Jack Bennett. I'm sorry if I've disturbed you at such an hour. I'm calling every number on my daughter's phone to see if I can find her."

"*Your* daughter is missing?" Caleb asked.

"She is out past her curfew. Actually, she was home but had snuck out of her bedroom. I'm calling around to see if anyone who knows her might tell me where she is."

"What's your daughter's name?"

"Mary Bennett. Have you spoken to her? Do you have a daughter who would know where she is?"

Caleb talked with Jack for a few minutes. It was assumed that both girls were probably together. Since the police told Mr. Bennett he couldn't file a missing persons report yet, they all decided to wait until the morning. It was agreed that if one of the daughters contacted any of them, they would phone each other.

Caleb said goodbye and hung up. He forgot to ask why Jack hadn't picked up the phone any of the other times they'd called his house in the last hour.

Caleb tried to talk Amelia into resting on the bed, but she refused to sleep until Sarah came home. Instead, she turned on the television and sat staring at it. Caleb figured she wasn't really tuning in to the retro game show blaring out how to win ten thousand dollars.

A half-hour later, he stepped into the living room to find her asleep, sitting crooked on the couch, her head dangling to the side.

He had been waiting for her to fall asleep. He had a phone call he wanted to make in private. There was a certain someone who might know where Sarah could be.

He made his way to the basement and dialed the number he had in his cell memory.

Chapter 19

Esmerelda rolled off her bed and knelt beside it. She stared along the narrow hallway of her trailer. She had heard something. A knock or a bang of some kind.

Then it came again, a soft rapping on the trailer door. A man called her name. She looked over at the digital alarm clock.

It read 3:14 a.m.

Who would be at her door at this hour?

She walked down the hall until she reached a window, parted the curtains, and looked out. She was reasonably sure whoever was standing outside wouldn't see her because she had no lights on.

It was the security guard from the gate. He had a teenage girl with him.

He knocked again.

Esmerelda opened the door. "Are you aware of the hour?"

"I know, and I'm sorry to bother you. It's just this girl." The guard turned and asked the girl what her name was. "Mary, here, says that she has information for you about your daughter. She says it's urgent."

Esmerelda looked past the guard and into Mary's eyes. "How do you know my daughter?"

"I don't know her. I just have something to tell you about her."

"Okay, like what?"

"Maybe we should talk in your trailer."

Esmerelda shook her head. "Whatever you have to say, you can say it out here."

"Sarah sent me. She's the one who told me to come to you about Denise

Hall, your daughter."

Esmerelda stepped back. Her fingers gripped the doorframe. No one even knew her daughter's name. After their falling out when her husband died, she stopped talking about Denise to anyone. It pained her too much to discuss her baby and how their relationship had been ruined. Most of her current friends weren't even aware she had a daughter.

The security guard turned to Mary. "Wait a second. You don't mean the same Sarah who broke in here this afternoon, do you?"

"I wouldn't know anything about that." Mary shook her head.

Esmerelda cut in. "It's okay." She edged past the guard and softly gripped Mary's arm. "Come on inside so we can talk."

Before shutting the trailer door, she thanked the security guard and bade him goodnight.

Esmerelda motioned for Mary to take a seat. She flicked on a table lamp beside the couch and looked back at her guest.

"Can I get you anything?"

"No, thank you."

Esmerelda came around and sat in her armchair opposite Mary. "Tell me what you came to tell me."

"I think Sarah is in trouble."

Esmeralda rubbed the sleep from her eyes. "I know that. I tried to warn her earlier."

"It's not just her, though. She said that Denise might get hurt, too."

Esmerelda sat back and absently started nibbling on a nail. "How would she know about Denise? How could my daughter be involved with Sarah?"

"I'm not exactly sure how it works. All I know is she gets told things about people. It's usually bad stuff. Things she has a chance to fix. Like when I met her—she saved me from being kidnapped."

Esmerelda sprang forward. "She saved you? Are you saying she gets these messages and changes the future? Is she actually doing something about it? That is so risky, even dangerous."

Mary went on to tell her about how Sarah intervened six months ago and saved her from being kidnapped and how she offered Sarah her phone number with a promise to repay her in any way she could. Sarah hadn't used the number until yesterday when she called for help.

"Sarah was on her way to stop another kidnapping. It would be late before she got home, and she asked me to text her parents saying she was sleeping over. That way, she could get home after midnight. If they asked what happened, she would tell them that we'd fought, and she'd decided not to stay."

"Did you send the text?" Esmerelda asked.

Mary nodded.

Esmerelda grabbed the hands-free phone. "We have to call the police. We've got to tell them what we know."

"Wait, no. Sarah explicitly asked us not to involve the police."

Esmerelda's thumb hovered. "Why? They're already investigating a hit-and-run on Birk Street. A witness said it was Sarah Roberts who drove the car."

"How do you know that?"

"It was on the news a few hours ago."

"Sarah said she wouldn't be as effective if everyone knew who she was. She said that helping people has given her purpose after years of depression. She doesn't want to stop."

"Wow, she told you a lot."

"She even admitted that. She said she'd never really trusted anyone before, but lately, she's been nervous about her own safety. She said you might be able to help. She also told me to tell you that Denise is your daughter and that she will be shot either today or tomorrow."

"That's it. I'm calling the police."

Chapter 20

SARAH STIRRED TO CONSCIOUSNESS. Everything ached. Her wrists and ankles were shackled to a heavy iron bed frame in one of the two rooms of the cabin. She had spent the night falling in and out of sleep on the hardwood floor.

Sunlight streamed through the room's storm window, too bright to look that way. She guessed it was about six in the morning by the sun's low angle.

The cabin was silent. She shifted and moved but couldn't find even a moderately comfortable position.

An old desk and a wooden chair sat in the corner by the window. On top of the desk sat a small stack of paperback books. She leaned forward and slid the handcuffs up the iron rod to the top.

She looked through the storm window, her eyes squinting in the sun at a wall of trees a hundred yards away.

Something sparkled in the sunlight on the window ledge. She pushed against her restraints to get a better look. A screwdriver sat on the windowsill sideways, a couple of screws beside it.

She then understood the situation in the cabin. Her captor planned on keeping his intended victim here. He hadn't just nailed the windows shut; he had screwed them down.

She needed to get her hands on that screwdriver.

The strain on her wrists was becoming more than she could bear. She dropped back to her knees and rolled onto her side.

The door to her room banged open.

"What're you doing?" her captor asked.

Sarah didn't say a word. He was unshaven and had bloodshot eyes. It looked like he was going through something internally that was driving him mad. She was sure at any moment that he would start foaming at the mouth.

"You think you're smart? You're in here moving around, trying to get those restraints undone. Well, let me help you."

He rushed over, dropped down, and produced a key. In seconds, Sarah was free. She scampered on her butt up against the wall by the window. She wanted to show fear. She also wanted to grab the screwdriver when he turned his back. Maybe he would give her enough time to drive it into his back.

"I undid you so you can come out, use the bathroom, and eat. Then you're tied up and in the trunk again. We're on the move. If you hear me tell you to stay quiet, you do it. Trust me, if you try to signal anyone, you'll cost them their life, and you'll pay that debt in pain. Do I make myself clear?"

Sarah nodded.

"Answer me! *Do I make myself clear?*"

Startled by his outburst, she stuttered in her compliance.

She was pulling again. One look at her fingers revealed hair as it fell from them. It had become an unconscious activity.

He looked at her, bewilderment creasing his brow. "What is the matter with you? Why are you missing all that hair? You got cancer or something?"

Sarah shook her head.

He walked over to her. "Go to the bathroom. Let's go. Last chance for a civilized rest stop." He said this last part with his arm pointed at the door.

She had no chance to grab the screwdriver now. He had not taken his eyes off her the whole time.

Ten minutes later, after using the bathroom to clean the caked blood on the back of her neck and readjust her bandanna, she ate sandwiches at a wooden table in the kitchen.

Her captor watched her intently, his eyes hardly leaving her. After an hour, he told her he would make a phone call and that he would be outside the cabin door. When he finished the call, they would be leaving.

She had to get to the back of the cabin, grab the screwdriver, hide it somewhere, and get back to the table before he noticed.

He stepped out and secured the door behind him. She jumped from her chair and bolted to the back of the cabin, even as her rusty joints shot pain through her legs. She rushed through the door to *her* room, ran to the window, and grabbed the screwdriver, holding it to her chest.

She had to get her breathing under control.

The cabin door banged open.

Shit!

She started to move, to hide, but stopped. The screwdriver was still in her hand.

He yelled for her.

She spun into a corner of the room and jammed the tool in the right front pocket of her jeans. Before her hand came out, the screwdriver nicked the inside of her palm.

She knelt, leaning against the wall.

He entered the room fast, a gun in his hand.

Sarah ducked her head and covered it with her arms.

"What're you doing in here?"

He didn't wait for an answer as he crossed the room and checked the integrity of the window. He turned to her and placed his gun against the skin of her temple.

"Are you fucking thick? Do you have a death wish?"

Sarah looked away, trying to show him that he cowed her.

"Get up," he ordered.

She remained on her knees. She didn't want to stand in front of him for fear he would see the impression the screwdriver made on her jeans.

"I said, get up."

She shook her head. Then he lifted her by the back of her shirt and shoved her through the bedroom door.

She fell hard, landing on her stomach before getting her hands out in front to absorb the fall. She grunted as the tool in her pocket jabbed hard just below her hips.

"I can see you'll need to be taught a few lessons. When I say something, you do it, or you get hurt. Understood?"

She nodded.

"Now, get up."

She struggled to get to her knees and then to her feet, keeping the pocket with the screwdriver out of his direct eyesight.

"Good. It appears you can learn a thing or two. Now walk. Go to the car and stand in front of the trunk."

When she got outside, he popped the trunk and motioned for Sarah to get in. She tried angling herself to avoid the tool in her pocket doing any further damage.

She felt his hands on her back. He shoved her hard and fast.

She had time to duck her head but cried out in pain when she banged her right shoulder against the top of the trunk.

The trunk lid came down, but not before she saw him smiling.

Evidently, my pain pleases him, she thought.

He had forgotten to tie her up in the chaos of leaving the cabin.

She twisted, bent, and straightened until she managed to pull the screwdriver out of her pocket.

Then she began working on her escape.

Chapter 21

Caleb started for the door. He would do it his way if he were to get his daughter back. The police didn't help when Vivian was kidnapped and murdered years ago, and he was convinced they would not be of much help this time either.

He stopped at the door. Did he really want to do this without Amelia? Would she understand what he was about to do? Could he tell her about the phone calls he had received and the ones he had made? Lately, it had always been a fight with Amelia. She had to do it her way. She would be hysterical if he told her what the caller said about Sarah this morning.

But maybe she *should* be let in on this.

He turned around and headed for the living room. His wife lay sprawled at a crooked angle on the couch, her neck twisted on the armrest.

"Amelia, wake up. It's nine-thirty in the morning. Sarah's still not home."

She grunted a reply and turned to ease the pressure on her neck. She massaged her jaw, wincing.

"What time is it?"

"Nine-thirty in the morning."

Amelia moved her head back and forth. He wasn't sure if she was saying *no* or trying to get the muscles moving again.

"I've got a splitting headache. Can you get me some Advil?"

Caleb was back a minute later with Advil and water. "Here, take these. Have a shower, and then we'll talk about what to do. I've called the plant and told them I wouldn't be in for a few days."

"Do you have coffee on?"

He looked at his watch. Every minute was important, and they were losing time. He couldn't wait.

"I made coffee. It's in the kitchen. Look, why don't you wake up, have a shower, and get dressed? I'll be back before you know it."

"Where're you going?" she asked, trying to look up at him, her head at a crooked angle.

The doorbell interrupted them.

"Stay here," Caleb said. "I'll get it."

He rushed to the door and saw two clean-cut men through the peephole. They looked like cops. One of them sported a goatee. Both wore suits instead of uniforms, making him think they were detectives. One man watched the street while the other stared at the peephole.

Caleb opened the door and lifted his hand to ward off the morning sun.

Goatee flipped through a notepad and asked, "Are you Caleb Roberts?"

Caleb nodded. "Yes. Can I help you?"

Have they found Sarah? Is she hurt? Or worse?

Both men identified themselves as police officers. "Would your daughter Sarah Roberts be home?"

"Not right now. Is there something I can help you with?"

Goatee looked at his partner and then back to Caleb.

"There was an incident downtown in the Entertainment District. A man was killed in a hit-and-run. Some witnesses put your daughter at the scene. If you know where Sarah is, it's in her best interest to meet with us so we can straighten everything out."

"A man was killed?" Caleb asked, stunned. Maybe that's why she didn't come home. She was probably in a jail cell. But then these guys would know that. "There must be a mistake because my daughter slept at a friend's house last night. I've got the text to prove it on my cell phone."

What had Sarah gotten herself into? Could she have killed a man?

"Can we come in?" Goatee asked and took a step forward.

Caleb blocked his way. "Right now wouldn't be the best time."

"And why would that be, Mr. Roberts?"

"It's my wife. She's not feeling well."

He'd decided earlier that he would not involve the police and was prepared to stand firm on that. If anything, they would bungle shit up. Caleb left Dolan a message last night after Amelia had fallen asleep. This morning he received a return call. Dolan was not going to help locate Sarah, even though that was *what he did*. Caleb had checked him out and learned he was renowned for his success rate in finding missing children.

The other call had been from the kidnappers telling him not to involve the police, or Sarah would die.

Today, the police would not be a part of his daughter's welfare. Caleb had other plans.

"I'm afraid that finding your daughter is a priority," Goatee continued, "and we would rather do that *with* your cooperation. So I need to ask if you're hiding Sarah?"

"Look, I understand I may appear a little apprehensive. It's just she's such a shy, introverted girl that I can't really believe what your witnesses said. What you are saying she's done is extremely unlikely. I'll talk to my wife. We'll make some calls. Leave me a number where I can reach you, and when we talk to our daughter, I'll get to the bottom of this, and then we'll contact you."

Goatee said, "It's not that simple. There's more to this than a car accident."

"What else is there?"

"We found a notebook at the scene."

Goatee turned and put his hand out. His partner placed a notebook in his hand.

"Do you recognize this?" Goatee asked. "Is this your daughter's notebook?"

Caleb nodded. He would recognize it anywhere.

"We scanned it and found references to kidnappings, accidents, and crime scenes." Goatee looked at Caleb, his face serious. "Information that only people investigating those crime scenes would know. In some cases, Mr. Roberts, she appears to know what is going to happen and when, *before* they happen, based on the dated entries. She's either psychic or plans the accidents and then tries to save people. We don't know what to believe here. Help us out."

Caleb couldn't control the quiver in his voice. "What are you saying?"

"There are references to Kim Wepps, a girl kidnapped and held for ten days not far from here. Based on her entries, we are starting to believe your daughter has some involvement in these kidnappings. Remember, this notebook was found at a murder scene where witnesses put your daughter, and we now have confirmation from you that it is, in fact, Sarah Roberts's notebook. Do you understand why we must find her before she does further damage?"

Could Sarah be a part of something this diabolical? Caleb closed his eyes for a moment.

"Tell him the rest," Goatee's partner said.

"We got a call a couple of hours ago from a woman who claims she is from the psychic fair in town. She told us that your daughter was in trouble, which we already knew. The odd thing was that she was also told that her daughter was in trouble. She says that her daughter will be shot in the next day or so. It looks like Sarah's planning something. We're going to have to find Sarah soon to stop this."

Goatee had opened the notebook to the last page of writing. Caleb saw *Dolan* circled numerous times in pen. *Save yourself* was written beside it.

He had wanted to find Esmerelda and make her fess up for the prophecy of danger she had given Sarah. He also wanted to talk Dolan into helping. Now he had no other choice. They had to come clean. They knew something.

A thought stirred in the back of his mind. Somehow, this whole thing had to do with the psychic fair. There was no doubt about it.

He gritted his teeth.

Dolan wouldn't even see him coming.

Chapter 22

SARAH HELD ON TO the screwdriver by its hard steel shaft as she shifted her position. Her hands slid along the smooth, velvety surface of the trunk liner until she came upon the plastic thumb screws directly behind the brake lights.

She removed all the thumb screws she could feel in the dark and then pulled the liner toward her, exposing the back of the brake light assembly.

Her tiny jail gained a small amount of light from outside. This helped her as she tugged on the brake wires, loosening the bulb.

"You awake back there?" her kidnapper asked.

She jumped and almost dropped the screwdriver when she heard his voice coming from the front of the car. She didn't answer him. She had no idea what difference it would make whether she was sleeping or not.

After a few moments, she heard him talking. She guessed he had wanted to make a phone call on his cell phone without her hearing anything. His quiet mumbling was not coherent when it reached her in the trunk. The sound of the highway racing by under the car was a steady drone.

With the bulb in her hand, she looked through the small hole where the brake wire had previously been. The red plastic brake light cover was all she could see. The hole was too small to accommodate her hand, which meant all her efforts were useless.

A Dead end. A small hole to nothing, she thought, hopelessly.

With the little light coming into the trunk, she started working on the lock mechanism with the screwdriver.

After at least five minutes, with nothing but sore hands, she gave up.

What can I do if I pop the trunk lid open while we're going sixty miles an hour on the open highway? she wondered.

The next time her kidnapper went to let her out, he would stumble upon what she did to the brake light and the trunk cover unless she could replace everything exactly as it was. That only made the situation worse.

The road got bumpier. The car hit a couple of small potholes, adding pressure to her shoulders. One was big enough to make her wince.

She took the end of the screwdriver and slid it through the hole where the brake light bulb had been. She applied pressure to the top corners of the outside red cover, trying to break it off.

More bumps hit the wheels. She rolled around for a better position and pushed harder. The floor of the trunk was merciless. Her right shoulder was on fire, the energy in her arm waning.

One corner popped loose, followed by another. From her limited view of the outside, she could see they were on a two-lane highway with little to no traffic.

They hit what felt like speed bumps in the road, big enough to jar her. The screwdriver got jammed and knocked from her hand just as the brake cover gave way and was lost to gravity. The screwdriver followed it out and onto the pavement behind the car. It clanged to the road and disappeared from view.

Shit, that was my only weapon.

Sarah angled herself to get a better look outside.

She could not believe the sheer coincidence when her eyes spied upon a police cruiser following them. She could only hope he pulled them over for a missing taillight. As much as she hated cops, this may be her chance to get away.

"What're you doing back there?" her captor asked.

Her stomach did a flip. She turned and looked at the underside of the trunk lid.

Gravel kicked the wheel well as he pulled onto the shoulder. Sarah dropped her head back to the hole she had made and saw the police car had its lights on.

The cop was pulling them over.

Here was her chance. This would all be over in minutes.

"I know you can hear me. Listen and believe me when I say I can make you die slowly. I will explore all of my sexual fantasies with you first. If you signal that cop, I will teach you the definition of torture."

She heard his car door open as he got out.

"What can I do for you, Officer?"

"I saw your brake light cover fly off. Thought I'd pull you over to let you know you also lost what looked like a screwdriver a little ways back there."

Sweat ran into Sarah's eyes. She raised her hand to wipe it away. Should she scream and take her chances? She barely breathed as she waited to see what would come next.

"Yeah, I knew it was loose. One of my errands in town was to get that fixed."

"Your plates say you're from Florida. That's a long way to head into town up here in Alabama."

Silence followed for a few seconds. Then Sarah felt her nerves vibrate her limbs when she heard the officer speak again.

"Open up your trunk. I want to get a look at that bulb."

Chapter 23

Caleb finished with the two detectives, closed the front door, locked it, and walked back into the living room. Amelia had not moved an inch. If Sarah was in real trouble, how would Amelia make it through the loss of another child? Could he count on her to be strong?

He looked at her with genuine concern, a part of him feeling sorry for her.

"Who was at the door?" she asked.

"Jehovah's Witnesses. It was hard to get them off the porch. Two guys with all these questions about religion."

"Is there anything new about Sarah? Has she called from Mary's?"

"Nothing yet, but I'm going to jump in the car and go find her."

Amelia used the back of the couch to get into a sitting position. "Where're you going to go?"

"I'm not sure yet," Caleb lied. Then he thought better of it. "I think I'll give that psychic fair a visit."

Amelia shook her head. "Sarah wouldn't be there. That's the last place she would be."

"What are you going to do?" Caleb asked.

Amelia picked up the remote control and flipped the television on. Caleb watched as she turned the volume low and searched for the local news.

"I'm going to get rid of this headache and start making phone calls, I guess. I'll start with Mary's dad and then work through Sarah's few friends."

"Why don't you call hospitals? Maybe she was admitted somewhere last night."

He looked away as Amelia glared at him. "You seem full of all the answers this morning. Why don't you call the hospitals?"

"Because I'll be in the car, driving around."

"Are you okay, Caleb? Let me rephrase that. Are we okay? Are we acting like parents with a daughter that didn't come home last night?"

"What do you think?"

"I look at your hands, and they're shaking. You're fidgety, moving around like you can't stand still. It's okay, you know. We'll get our Sarah back."

"How can you be so sure?" Caleb asked. "Are you aware of something I'm not?"

"You know I'm not. I just don't want to overreact. I need the first hour of the day to be calm for this splitting headache."

Caleb couldn't hold it in much longer. How could she be so selfish? Their daughter did not come home last night. The police were looking for her for crimes he was sure she had nothing to do with.

He didn't want to think about the other call he had received from the kidnappers earlier telling him not to involve the police. For his daughter's life, he would keep the police out of this as long as he could.

"You must ask yourself what you're doing as a parent to get your daughter back. What kind of commitment are you willing to make?"

"What are you talking about now?" Amelia's eyes didn't leave the news channel. "You know that I would do anything for Sarah."

"So get up and start doing something." His voice came out louder than he intended.

He didn't want to attack her. He wanted to weep at how unfair life was. He wanted to laugh at the craziness of it all. How could he have two daughters and both get kidnapped? A memory of something someone said years ago came back to him: *looking back on the tears makes you laugh, and looking back at the laughs makes you cry.*

He needed to leave as soon as he could. Every second counted.

"You're not being yourself," Amelia said. She set down the TV remote. "I think the first phone call I'll make is to the police department to see if they heard anything about Sarah."

"No! Don't do that," he shouted louder than he intended. "I'm stopping there first. It's only seven blocks away. You and I both know the amount of paperwork we must fill out on a missing person, which you can't do on the phone."

"Then I'll join you," Amelia said as she rose from the couch.

"No. You stay home."

Amelia stopped. She rubbed her temples in circles. "Why's that?"

"In case Sarah calls or someone else. Just promise me one thing." Caleb walked over and grabbed her arms above the elbow. He stared into her eyes. "Promise me you won't involve the police yet. You remember how badly they bungled the case with Vivian. Let me handle them for now. Okay?"

Amelia nodded.

Caleb grabbed his car keys and ran for the door without another word.

Chapter 24

An uncomfortable silence filled the trunk. A car whooshed by on the highway.

The heat seemed to be rising. It was getting unbearable.

She braced herself as she heard a key slide into the lock.

That's funny. He used the fob to open the trunk earlier.

She heard a soft thumping sound.

"Ah, man. I must've turned a little when I saw that car go by. The key broke in the fuckin' lock."

"Step aside," she heard the cop say.

Now she knew why he chose to use the key.

"You don't have to get uptight. I just broke my key."

Sarah could hear the agitation in her captor's voice. Something was about to happen. She pushed herself to the back of the trunk and closed her eyes.

"Wait for me here. I've got pliers in my cruiser."

Another car whooshed by.

A few moments later, she heard the pliers at work. Metal protested as she listened to one of them working on the broken key. Not ten seconds later, a horizontal light creased what little darkness was left in the trunk. A soft blast of cooler air brushed her cheeks as the trunk opened.

She looked up. No one was there.

There were sounds of a scuffle. She pushed the trunk lid all the way open and sat up. Too much light came too quickly. She had to rub her eyes and squint.

The men were fighting on the shoulder of the highway. It looked to Sarah like they were struggling for the gun that was now out of the cop's holster.

She climbed out of the trunk and fell to the ground. Her legs weren't ready for the weight.

A shot rang out. Sarah instinctively ducked.

She wanted to help the officer but was in no shape to do so.

She looked around to see if she could get someone's attention. Up and down the highway, she saw only one car, and it was traveling away from them.

She thought about the police cruiser. It would have a police radio and maybe another weapon.

She hobbled to the cop car. The driver's side door was unlocked. She swung it open and pushed herself into the driver's seat.

This kidnapping is over!

The thought brought a burst of energy with it. A laptop perched on a stand attached to the dash, a shotgun bolted to the dash beside it. The radio would be her best bet.

Sarah locked herself in the police car and started pushing the radio buttons.

Something hit the windshield. Sarah jumped backward and smacked her head on the headrest.

There was a bullet hole in the glass. The guy who'd kidnapped her was standing in front of the car, aiming the gun at her.

"Get out," he said. "Or the next one goes in your head."

Sarah unlocked the door slowly and eased it open. She got out cautiously and stood beside the cruiser on legs that couldn't be trusted.

"Now get in the back seat."

She moved toward the car they'd been in, the trunk still wide open.

"No," he shouted, waving the gun at her. "The back seat of the cruiser, you *fuck*."

She stopped abruptly, turned around, and got in the back of the cop car. The front door still sat ajar. She heard him ask the cop for his car keys. She couldn't see the officer from the back seat. Her captor still held the gun out in front of him.

She leaned back. There had to be another way out of this. She had been so close.

She could barely hear the cop ask, "What about me?"

Her captor shrugged, a shitty grin on his face. "Wrong place at the wrong time."

Sarah reached for the door handle. She had to make a run for it.

The gun went off.

Twice.

Chapter 25

BY THE TIME CALEB made it to the psychic fair's parking lot, he was fuming. To remain calm, he had been reciting his new mantra, *no police, no police.*

People gathered near the entrance doors. The fair looked busier than when he was here to pick up Sarah. He wondered if he would get a chance to speak with Dolan. Then he smiled at such a thought. Of course, he would. Dolan would be unable to refuse him, not after he found out his name was in Sarah's notebook.

He got in behind a small crowd and waited in line. Once he got to the ticket table, he bought a pass and swung the doors open to the fair.

He saw Esmerelda right away. She stood by a booth he guessed was hers. A girl about Sarah's age stood talking to her. Neither one saw him as they turned away and started down the aisle heading in the other direction.

Halfway down the aisle, he caught up with them.

"Tell me what's happened to Sarah," he said from two feet behind Esmerelda's back. "You can start with your prophecy of danger and then tell me where she is." Not knowing what to do with his hands, he crossed his arms across his chest.

Esmerelda turned around to face him. "If I knew where your daughter was, I wouldn't just tell you, I'd inform the police, too."

"We don't want the police involved," Caleb said.

Esmerelda looked at her companion. Caleb turned to her. "Who are you?"

"My name is Mary Bennett."

Caleb unfolded his arms and pointed a finger at her.

"You sent me a text last night."

Mary looked at Esmerelda, then back to Caleb. She nodded.

"What is going on here?" Not worried about making a scene, he shot out questions. "What have you people done? Who are you? Where do you have my daughter? I want answers." Spittle shot from his mouth as his agitation rose.

Both women backed away. It looked to Caleb that Esmerelda wanted to say something.

"Tell me where Sarah is," he said.

An audience had gathered. People stopped what they were doing to watch.

Esmerelda looked past his shoulder. Caleb spun around in time to see two security guards approaching.

"Look, I want my daughter. What is it? Money? Is that what you want? Just tell me."

"I'm on your side," Esmerelda said. "I'm not the enemy. I don't know who took Sarah, and I don't know where she is."

"Then explain the text I received. Why would you send it?" He stared at Mary.

He felt hands touch his arms. He twisted violently to release the grip.

"Don't touch me," he said in a deep snarl.

"Okay, mister, just calm down," the guard on his right said.

People were everywhere, edging closer. He even saw two teenagers with cell phones pointed at him, no doubt recording this for YouTube.

"My daughter was kidnapped last night. She warned us about it," he said, pointing at Esmerelda. "While this kidnapping took place, I received a text from her." He pointed at Mary. "But they won't tell me where she is."

The guard stepped forward, halfway between Caleb and the two women.

"I'm sure there's an explanation. Why don't we go to the office and sit down? We can all talk about it there."

"No. I'm not going anywhere with you people. I want to know where my daughter is right now."

Esmerelda stepped forward. "I already told you, I have no idea. No one here does."

"You sound like a lawyer. Don't worry. I won't sue. Just tell me where she is before I lose my fucking temper," Caleb said.

"Okay, mister. Let's go."

Both guards tried to manhandle him. Caleb wasn't as agile as he used to be, but he managed to get out of their grip. He swung his weight, planted a foot, and used his shoulder to knock the guard on his right off balance. Then, staying low, he whirled around and knocked the other guy off his feet. He hit him square in the stomach, the wind rushing out of his mouth.

"Leave me the *fuck* alone. I came here to find my daughter. I will not lose another daughter."

One guard tried to catch his breath while the other had both hands in the air, chest high. He nodded. "Okay, okay, take it easy," he said.

"What seems to be all the fuss here?"

"Who're you?" Caleb snapped at a tall man approaching from behind Esmerelda.

"My name is Dolan Ryan. I run this fair."

"Then you're the one I want to talk to," Caleb said. He pointed at Esmerelda. "Your psychic here is somehow involved in my daughter's disappearance, and so are you. My daughter wrote your name down in her notebook. The same notebook the police have in their possession. That's why I'm here."

"Why don't we go to my office?"

There were too many people surrounding them. Maybe Dolan and Esmerelda would say more behind closed doors. Caleb nodded.

Dolan walked away. Caleb followed him to an office in the back. One of the two guards came inside, and before shutting the door behind him, Esmerelda and Mary slipped in, making the office seem small with so many people.

Caleb filled Dolan in on the warning from Esmerelda and the text he received from Mary. Esmerelda told them about Sarah being on the news, and Mary explained why she sent the text and how she knew Sarah.

After everything was out, Caleb was dumbfounded. He'd had no idea who his daughter was or what she had become. He knew Amelia would not know that Sarah was out saving strangers from trouble. He told them about the police coming to his door this morning looking for Sarah.

"How do you explain your name in her notebook?" Caleb asked Dolan.

"We bumped into each other here at the fair. I saw my name in her book, too. I asked Esmerelda about it, but we couldn't come up with any reason why."

"If my daughter writes down some kind of prophecies and then acts on them, it would make sense that you're involved in some way. Your name was circled."

Everyone was silent for a few heartbeats. Caleb wondered if it had anything to do with Vivian. Maybe he closed down emotionally after she was murdered and hadn't been available for Sarah. He felt he had let her down, which motivated him even more to find her.

While everyone talked, Caleb couldn't help but think about where he was. His daughter was missing, and he was in a room with self-professed psychics.

He turned to Dolan. "Why don't you help? You've done this sort of thing before. There has to be a reason Sarah wrote your name down. Maybe it was a cry for help. Can't you use some psychic power to conjure up an image of where Sarah might be?"

Dolan shook his head. "It's not that simple. I'm retired. I know it's not what you want to hear, but I'm not the police."

"Why would you retire? It seems to me if you've got a God-given talent, you should use it."

Dolan stood. "If you must know, I'm sick of the notoriety. I'm old, and I can't handle the people anymore. I just don't want to. The police will just have to find all their missing persons with real old-fashioned investigative work."

To Caleb, Dolan's reasoning was selfish. "That's ridiculous. Listen to yourself. My daughter is missing, and you say you won't help, especially after it started here."

"What started here?" Dolan asked. "What *exactly* started here?"

The office door swung open, hitting the guard standing in front. He moved out of the way as a man walked in, followed by two uniformed police officers.

The mantra came back to Caleb. *No police.*

Dolan spoke first. "Alex, what's this?"

"Your security guard called them. After the break-in yesterday by his daughter, then the prowler at Esmerelda's trailer last night, security thought it better to have the police deal with him."

The man was pointing at Caleb.

"Hey, look," Caleb said, raising his hands in supplication. "I'm dealing with this amicably now. The story isn't so mixed up after all."

"Doesn't matter. You still assaulted the security guards."

"They grabbed *me*," Caleb said, exasperated, his patience thin.

One of the cops stepped closer to Caleb and nodded at Dolan. Apparently, the two men knew each other.

"Come with us," the cop said, motioning to Caleb.

Caleb wanted to run. If whoever had Sarah saw him with the police, it would be all over.

"No," was all he could think to say.

The air thickened.

"There's the easy way or the hard way," the cop said.

"I pick the hard way," Caleb said for Sarah.

Chapter 26

Amelia lifted the phone. Her efforts had proven fruitless. It had been thirty minutes, and she had gotten nowhere. One more hospital to call, then she would call the police. She refused to wait any longer.

The doorbell rang. She placed the phone back in its cradle and stood.

Could this be news about Sarah or Sarah herself?

She walked to the door like a zombie, the remnants of her headache an echo in her skull. When she got to the door, she straightened her shirt, pulled her shoulders back, and opened it. She was as ready as she would ever be.

"Can I help you?" she asked. A dark blue sedan sat parked in her driveway. Their family had lived next door to a cop in their previous home, so she could spot an undercover cruiser anywhere.

The tall man cleared his throat. "My name is Sam Johnson. I'm the lead investigator in last night's hit-and-run fatality. I'm sorry to intrude, but would you be able to furnish us with a current picture of your daughter?"

Amelia stepped back and frowned, her stomach flipping. Her knees got weak, and she felt lightheaded.

Fatality? What was he talking about?

"I'm not sure I understand what you're talking about. Is Sarah hurt?"

The officer made an odd facial gesture. His eyebrows raised like he was surprised. He took a step and looked at the number on the house. "Are you Amelia Roberts?"

Amelia nodded.

"I had two officers come by here earlier to explain what happened on Birk Street last night and to talk to your daughter. They met with your husband but forgot to ask for a picture. It seems the witnesses' descriptions have been inconsistent. If you could just furnish me with a picture, that would be very helpful."

Amelia wavered, grabbing the door handle for support.

"Is everything okay, ma'am?" the cop asked.

"Is Sarah … dead?"

The officer tilted his head to the side. "Not that we're aware of."

"You said fatality."

"A man was run down by a vehicle on Birk Street. Witnesses said the driver was your daughter. We went over this with your husband. He didn't tell you?"

Amelia shook her head enough to welcome the headache back. "He said it was Jehovah's Witnesses at the door."

"I'm sorry to hear that." He looked at his partner and then back at Amelia. "Why would he lie to you, Mrs. Roberts?"

"He didn't say anything about police." Amelia raised a hand to her forehead. "I need to sit down. Come in." She left the door open and made her way to the couch in the living room.

"Is there anything I can do? Would you like me to get you some water?"

"No. Just tell me what your men told my husband."

She sat back and listened while the detective walked her through what he knew about last night.

"And Caleb knows all this?"

"Yes. They even showed him your daughter's notebook. Can you tell me anything about this notebook? Was Sarah in and out at odd hours? Did she ever talk to you about it?"

So Sarah wasn't lying about not having her notebook. The police have it.

"No. She was quite secretive." Amelia leaned forward, put her elbows on her knees, and massaged her temples. "I just can't believe this. There's no way Sarah's involved in any sort of criminal activity."

"First, we need to locate her, and then we'll be able to ascertain what's really going on. You have to understand, Mrs. Roberts, from our point of view, that notebook has details … well, I don't want to jump to conclusions, but …" He left it hanging.

Amelia looked at him. "Don't, then. Don't jump to conclusions. Sarah is not involved in any crimes."

"We can't confirm that until we talk to your daughter. Although, it could be that she *was* helping people. We're just not sure. We've been provided with photographs from reporters in the past, including photos—from two separate occasions—featuring someone we believe was the person who'd intervened. Each time, that individual saved a life and then disappeared. And then that news anchorwoman was saved by a girl about your daughter's age. She was wearing a bandanna. There's a possibility it was your daughter, ma'am."

Amelia's thoughts wandered. "I thought, wait, my husband told me he was going to the police station. He said a missing persons report would be easier to file in person." She stood, not knowing what to do next but wanting to do something.

The cop stared at her. "A picture would really help."

"Right. Of course."

Amelia went to her photo albums and withdrew a picture from a few years back. Since Sarah had started *losing* her hair, she had refused to have any pictures taken. Amelia had snapped one while they were on a four-day mini vacation in Florida. Sarah had only started pulling her forearm hair and eyebrows at that time.

She returned to the living room and gave the picture to the cop. Tears crawled down her cheeks as the reality of the situation set in. She wiped at them and sat on the couch.

The detective studied the picture briefly and then slipped it into his jacket pocket. "I'd like to monitor your phones—if she *is* in trouble and gets a chance to call, at least my guys might be able to trace it. Would you mind if I had a couple of technicians come in to set up a tap?"

Amelia closed her eyes and nodded.

"There's a bit of paperwork to sign."

She opened her eyes in time to see him pull out a cell phone. He spoke fast, talking to someone about getting things set up.

She rose from the couch and ambled toward the kitchen for a glass of water. She was suddenly very thirsty. Her headache was gone. It had been replaced by a different ache.

Could Sarah really have driven a car that killed a man?

Amelia wondered if she was going to be sick.

Why did Caleb lie? What is happening to my family?

There was a soft knock on the kitchen door. She told him to come in.

"They should be here within a half hour. I'll have a little paperwork for you to sign."

The house phone rang.

Amelia grabbed at it. She answered before she heard any of the muffled warnings coming from the cop.

"Hello, hello, Sarah?"

"No, I'm sorry. My name is Dolan Ryan. I'm with the psychic fair."

Amelia almost hung up. She even saw herself slamming the phone down. She'd had enough of these people from the fair. "This isn't a good time."

"I understand. I'm aware of Sarah's troubles."

"You are? How's that?" She looked up at the cop standing a few feet away.

"Your husband was just here," Dolan said. "He explained everything. I thought the least I could do was give you a call to tell you that."

"Is my husband there with you?"

"That's why I'm calling. Your husband isn't here. He was taken away by the police."

Chapter 27

He tapped the steering wheel with his fingers.

This isn't going to work. It's not supposed to be this way.

He looked in the rearview mirror.

Every cop in the state will be looking for this police car soon.

He would have to make her pay. But she was too ugly to do anything fun with. He had promised himself he would have a little fun with the next girl they took, but not with this one. He could not get past all the missing hair. Whenever he looked at her body, all he could think about was a nuclear bomb survivor.

"What happened to you, anyway?"

She didn't answer him. He looked in the rearview mirror at her.

"I asked you a question. What happened to your hair?"

She continued to look out the side window.

"Fuck you, then."

"It's a disease. It's contagious," Sarah said.

He shook his head. *Yeah right.*

He passed another gas station on the right. That was two within the last ten minutes. No cop cars in sight. He looked in his rearview mirror. No one was following him.

He wondered if the cop had radioed in his position when he did the traffic stop. Could a broken taillight be important enough to call in the stop?

He saw buildings coming up ahead. A small town soon became visible. The sign said population 11,000. It also said *where daisies grow*. He chuckled to himself. The bitch sitting behind him would be pushing some up soon.

Doubt taunted him. He realized he probably wouldn't be able to pull this thing off. His brother was the one who always handled the details. He didn't know what to do next. Where would he go? Where did he think any kind of ransom money would come from?

A cop was dead, and here he was, driving through the town where the officer probably patrolled. People might recognize the car and wave, expecting the cop to be driving.

He swore loudly, smashed his hand against the steering wheel, and dropped lower in the seat.

He was making too many mistakes. The boss hated mistakes. He should have loaded the cop's body in the trunk—it might have delayed things a little. Instead of looking for a cop killer, they would be looking for the cop first.

Too late now, he thought, angry with himself.

He needed to think things through better.

Number one priority: ditch the cop car. He thought about killing the bitch but decided to keep her alive for now. He may need her to get out of a sticky situation. Maybe he could use her against the boss. Blackmail the boss to pay him hush money or have the girl go to the cops with all the information needed to put the boss away for a long time.

There, a plan was formed. Maybe he could clean this mess up after all.

He had to get out of this small town first. Everyone probably knew everyone else, and they wouldn't recognize him behind the wheel of the cop car. That would mean more witnesses telling where they saw the car later.

He ducked down just enough so he could still see over the dash.

Moments later, he came to the edge of town and passed the last house. He looked in the mirror and spotted the girl scrunched up in the back seat, her knees drawn to her chest.

"This is your fault," he said. "Things would have been easier if you had minded your own business. Who sent you, anyway? How did you know about our plans both times?"

She didn't respond.

"Did you hear me? When this is over, you die. You do know that, right?"

He rounded a corner and saw what looked like an old motel. From what he could see, the place appeared to be abandoned. He pulled off the two-lane highway and stopped in front of the rundown building. A sign said the area was slated for demolition. That would explain some of the construction equipment and the small white trailer on the side.

He pulled away from the front and drove around back, parking the police cruiser away from the view of the highway. He had been in police cars before, so he knew there was no need to worry about the bitch in the back seat. She could only get out when he opened the rear door from the outside.

The back of the motel looked like it had some work done recently.

That's strange, he thought. *Why renovate this dump when they're going to demolish it?*

He stepped out of the cruiser and scanned the gravel and mud driveway. There were no recent tire tracks or footprints—at least none since the last rainfall.

The last place to look was the construction trailer. Having arrived in a cop car, he walked around the motel and strode toward the trailer with authority. If someone saw him, they might assume he was undercover as he wasn't wearing a uniform.

The door to the trailer was locked. He looked in the window to the right of the door. No one was in sight.

Perfect.

He could use one of the abandoned rooms to keep the girl for a day or two. Since it was a Friday night, he figured no one would come back to work here until at least Monday. He would be long gone by then. *Long gone.*

He jogged back toward the cruiser. Five meters from the cop car was the edge of a steep hill. It ended where a small lake started.

Things were looking up.

He turned, opened the rear door, and pulled the girl out. She sat on the grass and stared off into space, her face blank. Her right hand was at the nape of her neck. He leaned over to see what she was doing. Her thumb and index finger were yanking on a small clump of hair. He twisted his face up and stepped away from her.

Her fingers fluttered behind her head, hair dropping from them.

He shook his head. *Fuckin' weird.*

He shifted the cruiser into Neutral. Then he began to push, which was easier than he thought.

The vehicle crested the top of the hill and started its descent. On the way down, it bottomed out a few times, scraping against large stones and gouging small holes into the earth.

It hit the bottom of the hill and smacked into the water with a huge splash. Then it started its slow descent to the bottom of the lake.

He turned back to the girl on the grass.

She was gone.

Chapter 28

Amelia could hear the detective summoning her from the den.

"Mrs. Roberts, I think you'd better come to listen to this."

After talking to Dolan, she needed a few minutes to herself before she told the cops that her husband was at their police station.

The sun shone through the blinds covering the front window. Amelia stared at the floor where the light made curious straight lines and wondered if she was ready to hear whatever the cop wanted her to listen to. Could she handle it if something happened to Sarah? Why did she feel so weak, helpless, and vulnerable?

Maybe because within one day, my family has gone mad and fallen apart.

"Mrs. Roberts?" The detective stood in the doorway.

Amelia acknowledged him with a nod and started down the hall.

They entered Caleb's den, where two plainclothes officers were setting up wires and what she gathered were listening devices. Both men had been introduced to her earlier, but she had already forgotten their names.

"When we noticed messages on the machine, we decided to listen to them in case your daughter had called in. Anyone could've called when you were asleep and left information that might help."

"Okay." Amelia took a step back and leaned against the wall.

"How well do you know your husband?"

"What do you mean?"

The detective looked over at his technicians, made some kind of gesture, and turned back to Amelia. Both men stood and walked out of the room, closing the door behind them.

"What's going on here, Detective?"

"Sam. I would prefer it if you called me Sam. We'll spend a little time together, so it would be easier if you'd use my first name."

"What did you hear on the answering machine?"

"I don't want to alarm you. Maybe you should be sitting down for this."

"I'm not a baby. Just tell me. I can handle it, or at least I'll try to."

Perhaps he was right. If the worst news was about to come out of the machine's tiny speaker, maybe she should be sitting down. She dropped to the couch cushions and rested her face in her hands.

She heard a button being pushed and the familiar click of a message about to start.

Amelia identified her husband's voice immediately. He wasn't speaking from the phone in the den because the machine had picked up at the same time as Caleb and had inadvertently recorded the conversation she was about to hear.

"*Hello,*" Caleb said, his voice rushed as he ran for the phone.

A whispered response followed. "*I have your daughter. I want five hundred thousand delivered to a location I will reveal in ten days.*"

Amelia gasped. Sarah had been kidnapped. It was official now. Her baby had been taken. And her husband knew about it. Why hadn't he told her? Why hide it?

"*Who are you?*" Caleb shouted. "*How do I know you've got her?*"

"*You've got ten days. No police or she dies. No police.*"

Amelia heard a click and the answering machine stopped. She let out a breath she had been holding and raised a hand to cover her open mouth. Where was Sarah now? Was she safe? What could be happening to her?

"Mrs. Roberts? Do you need a moment?"

Amelia shook her head back and forth. *I have to be strong.* She adjusted her shirt, wiped her face, and addressed the detective.

"What time was that call recorded?" she asked.

"The machine time-stamped the message at 7:34 a.m. Your husband took the call before my officers came to your door this morning. That's probably why he told you it was Jehovah's Witnesses at your door. The caller said *no police.*"

She hoped Caleb's lie was to protect Sarah. "The call came when I was still asleep. Why wouldn't he tell me?" She drifted off with her thoughts.

"Maybe it was because he was headed to the psychic fair. He wouldn't have wanted me to know he was going there because he despised the place. We've argued over the past week about that fair."

"What did you argue about?" the detective asked.

"I wanted to take my daughter there, and he didn't. Caleb doesn't believe in psychics of any kind. He probably went to see who was involved with Sarah's kidnapping because of the warning Esmerelda gave her."

"What warning?" the detective asked. "Who is Esmerelda?"

"When Sarah attended the fair, a psychic named Esmerelda warned her that she was in danger. That's why the police took him away. He was probably pissed off after the ransom call and headed there straight away thinking they had something to do with this."

The possibility of never seeing Sarah alive again hit her. She felt physically wounded. On the table beside the couch was a Kleenex box which she fumbled with until one came loose. She blew her nose and tried to compose herself.

"Mrs. Roberts, when you said the police took him away, what were you referring to?"

She looked at the cop. He was standing by the phone.

How did my life come to this?

She hugged herself when the thought came to her that she may have to bury another child. She would lose her mind if Sarah were killed.

It wouldn't be only Sarah dying. It would be a family.

Chapter 29

"I'VE DONE ALL THAT I'm going to do," Dolan said as he walked away from Esmerelda.

"Which is not nearly enough," Esmerelda said as she hurried to keep up. "We've known each other a long time. I've never seen you shrug off a kidnapping like this. Why, Dolan? Just tell me, why?"

"I already did. Too many lives are at risk. I feel my involvement adds to the level of danger."

"That sounds ridiculous. You don't really believe that, do you?"

She wanted his attention and knew the easiest way to get under his skin was to question his psychic abilities. They were walking through the back corridor leading to the employee parking lot. When Dolan got to his car, he would be leaving. That gave her a minute to persuade him to help Sarah.

"Look me in the eye." She stopped to catch her breath. "And tell me you are absolutely certain that you helping Sarah will do more harm than good."

He turned to face her. The pause gave her a chance to breathe. She leaned against the wall, panting, a hand on her chest.

"Esmerelda, why do you question me like this? You've seen me help so many people for over twenty years. I'm not a hero. But you know as well as I do that, number one, I can't save everybody, and number two, I shouldn't save everybody."

He stopped talking for a moment to let other employees walk past. He looked back at Esmerelda. "What I mean is, there are people who should live the path they're on without interference. Changing fate is a dangerous game. You, of all people, know that."

"I don't believe philosophy is the reason behind this. I think there's a personal reason. And I think you're being selfish." She pushed off the wall and stood to her full height, all four feet, eleven inches. "How popular you are with the public won't change whether you help Sarah or not. People will continue to treat you like a celebrity until you move to a remote mountain cabin and become a recluse. One more teenage girl won't change your life, but it'll change hers."

He turned and started for the parking lot again. She followed close behind as they stepped out onto the asphalt.

"Dolan, listen to me," Esmerelda pleaded. "I don't want to say this, but if you don't try to help Sarah, I will leave this fair. Do you hear me? I will quit. I can't stay here with the principles you're bound to."

He stopped walking. The sun bounced off something shiny on the pavement, causing her to squint.

"Esmerelda, you are being most difficult. Trust me when I say my lack of interference isn't personal. It's just …"

"What? What's stopping you? Tell me."

"I feel someone close to me is directly or indirectly involved with this case. I don't know how or why, or who this individual is. All I do know is if I *don't* help Sarah, this mystery person will live. On the other hand, this person dies if I get involved. I will be killing him or her by my actions, whether unintentional or not." He turned to face her. "I can't aid in Sarah's kidnapping case because I refuse to be a murderer."

Chapter 30

Sarah crouched low.

He would have been able to see her if she had gone for the highway. It was too wide open. The woods on either side would have given ample shelter, but getting to them posed the same problem: too far to get unseen.

So she had run in through the open back door of the motel. Maybe she could find a way to get to the front and then run for the highway. She had tried the dusty pay phone by the front counter, but it was dead.

When the motel owners had abandoned the building, they had taken everything with them, leaving Sarah nothing that could be used as a weapon.

She stayed low, hiding under a window that looked out to the back of the motel where the police car had gone over the edge of the hill. She watched as the guy realized he was standing on the brown grass alone. He turned and ran to the edge of the building, where he disappeared from sight.

She decided to venture outside. If the guy stayed in the front of the building, searching for her near the highway or in the woods, maybe she could get below the edge of the hill and be gone.

Glass broke in a room next to her. She jumped and covered her mouth. He sounded angry with all the noise he was making.

Her back hunched, she ran for the door that led outside. Just before she reached it, a large shadow filled the doorway. Sarah came to an abrupt stop. Sweat broke out on her neck and back. A lone strip of moisture glided gently down her spine. The man in the doorway wasn't her captor, but that didn't come as a relief.

He had some kind of automatic weapon in his hand. She heard more glass breaking behind her, followed by a man screaming.

"He kidnapped me," Sarah whispered. "Can you help me?"

The brute of a man reached in and grabbed her. He spun Sarah into him, almost enveloping her with his size. Her small struggle was futile, her verbal protests quieted by his large hand.

He pulled her outside with him. Half dragging, half lifting, he guided her to the construction trailer. Seconds later, they were inside, and the door locked behind them.

She wondered who he was and why he would carry a gun out in the open. He hadn't said a word, but it was an improvement because she wasn't with her captor anymore.

Maybe this is the end of my ordeal.

"Can I use your phone?"

He was on her with speed she didn't know someone his size could have. When he clamped his hand over her mouth, it was so large that it covered her nose, too. Her lungs fought for air as she scratched at the hand covering her face.

After a moment, he let her catch one breath and then sealed his hand on her mouth again. Using his teeth, he pulled off a small strip of duct tape. Air rushed to her lungs when his hand left her face just before the man took the strip of duct tape and covered her mouth. He laid her down and worked on her ankles and wrists until she was secured with the tape.

He nudged her hips with his foot to get her against a wall. Breathing fast through her nostrils, she watched him grab a blanket. He came back and covered her with it.

The world turned a soft green. She struggled and twisted, but the blanket remained. It lifted and dropped with her breathing. She couldn't hear much of what he was doing. Her pulse pounded in her head. She was thinking about dumb luck and how much of it she had. How could someone go from being kidnapped to being rescued by a kidnapper? It was insane.

A dark urge grew inside her—the need to pull. It blossomed into something uncontrollable, making her moan and writhe. The need to pull was always there. Sometimes it was soft and delicate. Other times, desirable, a pleasure. But this urge was a demand, one that she couldn't answer.

With the muscles in her arms straining, she wrapped her fingers around, testing the bonds of tape on her wrists. It was no use. She would not be able to pull any hair until someone undid her.

Her mind slipped. She felt a subtle kind of letting go. There was freedom in pain. There were also tears. One rolled down her cheek and fell into the recess of her ear, cooling as it settled.

She pinched a small piece of skin on the back of her hand, imagining it was hair she was removing. She pinched harder, hoping to calm herself.

Her moans increased.

Something hard hit her in the side of the head, knocking her into the trailer wall.

Consciousness swam away.

Chapter 31

Thoughts about tomorrow kept running around in Denise's head. Was everything worked out? Did they have all the precautions in place? Would Mr. Ward be a problem?

She hated dealing with people like Mr. Ward. He carried an attitude that stated his self-importance, living life as if he was on a stage. A drama fixed for the audience of his employees. He, however, was the man with the money. And she wanted this deal since it would be the last deal she made in this business.

She swiveled in her office chair and opened the bottom desk drawer. In it, a dated photo of her mother sat face up. It had been taken a year before her father died. The same year they stopped talking.

Her mother had been quite upset with Denise's decision to sell off the family heirlooms. A couple of generations of artwork were left to Denise in her father's will. Various collectors snooped around after Denise's father passed away, looking to determine who would control the small fortune.

Denise sold it piecemeal, living off the smaller, less expensive items for the first five years. Then she met Mr. Ward. He paid her top dollar for some of her father's collection. In the last fifteen years, Denise had sold almost everything.

It was rumored that the painting called *White Center* by a guy named Rothko would fetch millions at Sotheby's in New York if she had wanted to auction it. It was completed in 1950, and her father bought it for under a hundred thousand dollars by the late fifties.

The large seven-foot canvas had not been easy to transport without damage. She wasn't in the art business. She was only a seller. Fortunately, she had succeeded in the safe relocation. Now it sat in the secured and renovated shell of the Sky Blue Motel, guarded twenty-four hours a day by armed security—some of the best money could buy. There were reasons for it: the recent break-ins at Sotheby's and two other serious art dealers so keen to secure this painting for their private collections that they had sent men to threaten and intimidate Denise.

Denise had had her storage facilities broken into, as well. She had not been good at being discreet or security conscious. It had seemed better for her to keep the higher-priced stuff in warehouses and storage units than have it at her home. The threats and attempted thefts had helped to change her ideas on security.

This was her last piece that held notoriety, her ticket back to normalcy. Once it was gone, she would have nothing left for collectors to hound her for. Museums could take the rest. What did she care? Mr. Ward made her a generous offer that would keep the painting out of an auction house and her out of the poor house forever.

Staring at her mother's picture brought back a lot of memories. Maybe when this was all over, she would try to find her.

"Esmerelda." Denise said her mother's name out loud, digesting the sound of it in her ears.

She jumped when the phone rang, then snatched it up.

"Yeah?"

"We got a problem."

"What problem?"

"A cop was just here."

"A cop? What are the police doing there?"

"He pulled in and dumped his car. I've got the girl."

She wondered where these guys got their smarts. Half explanations were frustrating. She stood and turned to look out her office window. It opened to a garden surrounded by trees. *Calm*, she thought. *Stay calm.*

"What do you mean by *I've got the girl*? And why would a cop dump his car?"

"The girl he was traveling with. She ran into the motel. Jenkins and I scanned the perimeter, but the cop is gone. He just disappeared."

"Disappeared? Cops don't dump cars and disappear. Could it be he wasn't a cop?" She put a hand on her forehead. This was not good. Mr. Ward wouldn't do business with her if he knew the police were snooping around. It didn't matter whether it was a real cop or not. This could be bad.

"He disappeared. I would know if he was still here. I've tracked people before."

"Then ask the girl who he was and why they came to the motel."

"I can't."

Her frustration hit new levels. "Why can't you?"

"She's unconscious."

"Why is she unconscious?"

"I knocked her out to keep her quiet."

Great, Denise thought. *This had* horrible *written all over it*.

"Look, I can't be there until the transaction happens tomorrow morning. Keep the girl safe, and keep her out of the way until this is done. Can you do that?" A beep came through the line. Someone was calling her. "Hold for a second. Someone's calling me on the other line."

She pulled the phone from her ear, pressed the button, and said hello in too gruff a voice.

"Is something wrong?"

She collected herself immediately. "Not at all, Mr. Ward. What can I do for you?"

"I was calling to make sure our meeting is still on for tomorrow morning."

"It is. Everything's set. I'll have the account numbers for the wire transfers ready. The package will be prepared for transport."

"Good. I'll see you in the morning," he said and hung up.

She went back to the other line.

It was dead.

Chapter 32

The edge of town was close. Gert checked the signal on his cell phone and saw only one bar.

He needed direction. He needed to know what to do, and he needed someone to tell him. It was something his late brother would offer. Since he was dead, the boss would have to take his place.

He checked his phone again. Two bars.

He dialed the boss's cell phone number. He got a machine after five rings. He hit redial and waited. It was answered on the third ring.

"What's up? It's, like, two in the morning. Why are you calling now?"

"I got trouble." He heard his boss moving like he was getting out of bed.

"You're fuckin' right you do, Gert. What the hell were you guys thinking? I still can't get over the fact that you two didn't take the girl we'd planned on."

"Because *this* girl fucked that up. She got in the way. It was the second time she'd been at one of our kidnappings in six months. Too coincidental. She was trying to steal our car."

Gert heard his boss swear under his breath.

"I figured something was weird with her when I saw her at the psychic fair the other day. I thought it was the same girl you spoke about on the Bennett kidnapping. She looked as outlandish as you described, with all that hair missing in clumps. I called her house and tried to set up a meeting, but she hung up on me mid-sentence."

Gert stopped walking and turned from the shoulder of the highway. An SUV passed, making it difficult to hear well.

"I want the money for the kidnapping we were supposed to do," Gert said.

"You're kidding, right?"

"No. My brother was killed, and I won't let him die for nothing."

"Can you hear yourself? Do you know what you're saying? We can't do the ransom gig. You don't have the right girl. We know nothing about her parents' financial status. Kill this girl and dump the body in a swamp before every cop in the country is after you."

He shook his head even though he knew the boss couldn't see him. "No way. Put the money in the account, or I'll tell the parents who you are."

There was a pause before his boss spoke. "You don't want to threaten me. I could give the police your name and location, and they'd hunt you down. They wouldn't even ask me how I knew. They'd assume it was my psychic abilities."

He slowed his breathing. Better not to lose control. He needed help here, not an enemy.

"She's gone."

"What?"

"She's gone. The bitch escaped. I couldn't find her. I looked for an hour and then hunkered down in one of the rooms to wait in an abandoned motel. I fell asleep until after midnight. I've been walking back toward town ever since."

"You're lying. What motel? Where are you?"

Gert didn't know what to say. What if the boss wanted him dead? He couldn't tell him where he was. It was too risky.

His boss continued, "Go back and get her. She can identify you. Once you have her, get her to write something for you."

"What're you talking about, *write something*?"

"When I saw her at the psychic fair, she dropped to the ground and started writing in her notebook. I've worked with many psychics over the years, and I know she's an automatic writer. I think she's aware of the kidnappings because someone's telling her about them through her pen."

"Are you for real?" Gert asked.

"We need her off the street for good. She can identify us."

"Now I know you're *fucking* with me because there's no way she could have that information. Listen to you. There's no such thing as real psychics."

"I saw it. Believe me. That's why she has to die."

"Are you sure you don't want this one found safe like the other girls we've taken?"

"She told Esmerelda something important. I may have to remove her too. Everything is getting out of hand. Why did you have to take Sarah in the first place?"

Gert gripped the cell phone tighter to his ear as a loud rig passed by. "You actually believe this automatic writer shit?"

"You're asking *me* if I believe in psychic stuff. Come on, just do your fuckin' job and stop killing random people. I can't help you if they launch a nationwide manhunt. Don't make any more mistakes. The girl has to die. Go back to the motel and find her. After this blows over, we'll take a month off and hit another city. I'll get close to the investigation on my side to keep on top of their progress. I'll try to give them something psychic."

Gert ended the call as a fly buzzed his ear. He swatted at it and turned toward town. Instead of walking back to the motel, he needed to steal a car and drive around. It had already been a two-hour walk into town. He didn't feel like just turning around and going back.

He looked at the time on his phone. He could get back to the motel by 5:00 a.m., depending on how long it took to steal a car.

He could find the girl and be back on the road before the sun came up.

He would also need pen and paper to see if this automatic writing shit was real.

She would write something for him, or he would kill her. Easy as that.

His step felt lighter with the knowledge that Sarah would die today.

Chapter 33

Amelia heard the car approach and looked through the living room window as Caleb strode to the front door. He walked in and slammed it behind him.

"It's well past midnight. Where've you been?" she asked, even though she knew.

"What's all this?" His eyes seemed wild, panicked. "Why are you people in my house?"

"Why didn't you tell me about the ransom call?" Amelia asked.

He glared at her. "I didn't want to worry you. You went through enough when we lost Vivian. I wanted to check something out first. Then I was coming home to fill you in on everything."

Amelia stepped back.

"Why are the police here?" Caleb asked. "If you know about the ransom call, why are the police here?" He turned away from her. "Okay, everyone. This is my house, and I'm asking you all to leave right now. Gather your things and get out. This is a private affair."

Sam Johnson stepped into the room. "Hello, Caleb. We came because of the hit-and-run last night. We were looking for a recent photo of your daughter. Once your wife and I talked, we realized she didn't know about our earlier visit, so she invited us in. Now we're looking for your daughter the right way. No cowboy stuff. Trust me. This is the right way to handle this. We have been discrete if the kidnappers are watching the house, but we don't think they are."

"How can you be so sure?" Caleb asked.

"We've discretely checked every house on your street."

"How can you do that?"

"We pulled the deeds at the city to find out who owns them. Then we made a list of license plate numbers and matched the names up. After that, we took this information and all the pictures of the individuals who lived in each home and began a multi-team surveillance to see who was coming and going throughout the day. This takes about twelve hours before we can determine that each house is secure, except for the few where the owners are away on vacation. We have two men in the street minding those houses for movement. Everything else is under control."

Amelia knew the smile on Detective Johnson's face would not win her husband over. They had both lost a lot of respect for how the police did things when Vivian was taken from them. Vivian's killer was never caught.

"I don't like it," Caleb said. "I already lost one daughter, and I'm not going to lose Sarah. The person on the phone told me not to involve the police. I don't want you here, but I won't go so far as to tell you to leave … yet. Find my daughter soon, or get out."

Amelia looked at the detective. He nodded and turned away, leaving them alone.

"You said you wanted to check something out," Amelia said. "Then you were going to tell me about it. What was it?"

Caleb took her arm. He led her down the hall and into their bedroom.

"Are they listening in?" he asked.

Amelia shook her head.

"I don't believe in psychics, but I went to talk to Dolan Ryan. That's the guy who runs the psychic fair. If he's really some kind of psychic, then why not help us find Sarah?"

"You've changed. A week ago, you would have laughed at me if I had done the same thing."

Caleb nodded and looked at the floor. "I know. But after that fortune teller warned Sarah about danger and now this, I just thought maybe there was something to it. That's why I told you it was Jehovah's Witnesses at the door. I didn't want the police involved until I talked to Dolan."

"What did he say?"

"He said he wouldn't help us. Then the police took me downtown and said I had to stay away from the psychic fair. I got a cab back to the fair's parking lot to pick up our car. I've been driving around for the last I-don't-know-how-many hours, hoping to spot Sarah. I know it was stupid, but what else can I do? I feel useless."

The phone rang.

They looked at each other and then left the room. Halfway up the hall, Amelia saw Detective Johnson coming toward them with a hands-free phone held out.

Amelia grabbed it on the fourth ring.

"Hello?"

"Is this Mrs. Roberts?"

"Yes. Who's this?" She looked at the cop in the cramped hall. He nodded and rolled his hand in a gesture to keep going.

"My name is Dolan Ryan. You may remember me from my earlier call about your husband."

"Yes. Go on."

"I know about Sarah's disappearance."

"My husband just came home. He told me about your meeting today."

"Things have changed. When your husband and I met, I was letting personal reasons stop me from getting involved, but I think I know where Sarah is. I must speak with you right away."

Amelia almost dropped the phone. She fumbled with it and then secured it to her ear. "What did you say? If you know where she is, tell me."

"It's not that easy. The location is secluded. I need to debrief the police. They will have to send in a tactical unit. Let me work with the police, and I'll get your daughter back."

Chapter 34

It was after five in the morning, and he still had not found a car. The sun would be up soon. The delay complicated things. The girl could be anywhere by now. She could've hitched a ride or even walked back to town as he did.

It was stupid to leave the motel. Gert wondered why he did it in the first place. Would going back be worth it? She couldn't have made it far. She was weak, tired, and hungry. She had probably passed out in the motel somewhere, which meant she would awaken with the sun and have more strength after a long rest, giving her a good chance to make a clean break.

He had to go back to the motel as soon as he could get a car. He had to be sure.

He made his way to a three-story apartment building. Cars dotted the parking lot. He was hoping to find an SUV or van of some kind. Older models preferred as car alarms these days were difficult to circumvent.

Headlights cut through the early morning fog. A vehicle turned onto the street he was walking on.

Gert ran and dodged behind a row of trimmed bushes. He crouched down and waited for the car to pass.

He knew they would've found the dead cop back on the highway by now. No doubt there would be cops everywhere looking for the killer. Anyone found strolling the streets at this early hour would be questioned, and he didn't want to take any chances.

The car moved slowly, drawing closer. He figured it was still too dark for anyone to see him easily, and he wanted a good look at who was coming, so he chanced a peek.

The first thing he saw was the lights on the roof. A police car.

Then he had an idea. Why steal a random vehicle and have to hope he could get past the car's alarm? Why not just take another cop car? He would get more weapons, a police scanner so he could hear what other cops were up to, and he would look like he was transporting a criminal when he got the girl in the back seat.

He searched his jeans pocket to confirm he still had the fake police identification he had used for the girl on Birk Street.

Perfect.

He ran onto the road in front of the cop car. It jolted to a stop.

"Help! My wife is hurt."

The driver's side door opened, and the officer got out. He stayed behind the door.

"Put your hands on your head," the cop said.

Gert acted surprised and out of breath. "What? I just told you my wife is hurt. These guys knocked on our door twenty minutes ago and invaded our home. I managed to get away, but they got my wife. I need your help. Come on." He turned away as if to go, then stopped and looked back.

"I said, put your hands on your head," the cop ordered. "Do it now."

He raised his hands, trying to act the part of a distraught husband.

"Why are you fully dressed?" the cop asked. "You're always dressed like that at five in the morning during a home invasion? When you said 'managed to get away,' I'd expect you to be in pajamas or something."

Gert managed to get a tear out. It slipped across his cheek. "I was traveling back from visiting family. I got in late. I hadn't undressed for bed yet. My wife was asleep. They had weapons. I had no choice but to run."

He took a step toward the cruiser. The officer didn't challenge him but remained standing behind his car door. Gert could tell he was still suspicious.

"Where do you live?" the cop asked.

Got me, he thought. What was the name of the street he was just on? He racked his mind for a street name. To stall, he cocked his ear and asked the cop to repeat his question.

"Two blocks over," Gert said, pointing behind him.

The officer moved around the door of the car. He kept a hand suspended near his holster. "Step up to the vehicle and put your hands on the hood."

"Are you serious?"

"I said put your hands on the hood."

Gert shook his head and gave the guy his best I-can't-believe-you look.

He did as he was told, stepping up to the car and placing his hands on the hood. "You're something else, you know that? My wife could have been raped by now. I ran out to get help. Of all the luck, I find a cop. But now I'm being treated like a suspect or something."

He talked as the cop drew closer. Then he felt the cop's hands on him. Gert couldn't let the cop pat him down.

He closed his eyes. As the officer frisked Gert, his hand brushed the gun in Gert's waistband.

With as much speed as he could muster, before the cop had time to react, Gert spun around and jammed his hand into the cop's neck just below the jawline.

The cop had almost had his gun out of its holster, but now both his hands clung to his throat as he gasped for air.

Gert spun the cop around, took his gun, and then shoved him against the cruiser's hood. The cop bounced off the car and dropped like a large fish fresh out of the water, gasping for air.

He knew it wasn't a killing blow. A punch in the Adam's apple is awful, but unless the trachea collapsed, the cop would live. He needed to be careful about random killings.

The cruiser was still idling. Gert slipped behind the wheel and hit the gas. The forward motion slammed the driver's side door closed.

He looked in the rearview mirror. The cop was rolling on the ground, still holding his throat. It was hard to tell from this distance, but it looked like the cop was talking into a handheld microphone suspended on his lapel.

Shit.

He should've ripped that off him. He wasn't thinking fast enough.

Gert dropped the accelerator and raced the cop car out of town. He increased the volume on the police radio. Dispatchers were sending officers to a domestic and another to a traffic violation for backup.

The clock on the dash read five-thirty a.m. He would be back at the motel in twenty minutes or less.

He would find his girl and try for the state line.

Chapter 35

The morning sun shone brightly through her windshield. Even though Denise only had a mile left, she opened the console between the seats and pulled out her sunglasses.

It looked like she would arrive thirty minutes earlier than Mr. Ward. They would transfer the money, load the painting onto a special truck Mr. Ward was bringing, and the deal would be done. If everything went as planned, Denise would be free and clear within two hours. Then she would deal with the girl her guards had found.

She pulled into the Sky Blue Motel. No cars were visible. It looked like no one was there.

Perfect.

She stopped in front of the construction trailer and turned her SUV off. Her stomach was in knots. This was a legitimate sale, nothing illegal, yet she still felt like a criminal.

"It'll be over soon," she said out loud to comfort herself.

She got out of the vehicle and sucked in a deep breath. The smell of the pines made her think of being at a cottage.

The wooden steps of the construction trailer creaked under her weight as she fumbled with the keys.

A car on the highway slowed behind her. She turned to see a dark-colored Cadillac angling into the abandoned motel's parking lot. She waited until the vehicle stopped behind hers. Two men got out. They looked like Mr. Ward's thugs.

"Denise Hall?" the driver asked.

"Who're you?"

"We're the advance team for Mr. Ward. We're here to make sure everything goes smoothly."

The guy had a New York accent.

"I'm sure everything will, but suit yourself. Hang around or do whatever you want. He's not expected for a little while yet."

"You won't even know we're here." The driver smiled.

The two men got in their car. Denise watched as they drove around the side of the motel and disappeared behind it.

She had not expected the additional team.

She opened the door to the trailer and stepped in. Her head of security, Bruce, stepped out from behind a partition. The partition allowed the guards to use the trailer at any time without worry of someone looking in through the trailer window.

"Who were those guys in the Caddy?"

"Mr. Ward's men."

"Early."

"I know. Where's the girl?"

"Over here."

The guard stepped sideways and motioned behind the partition. Denise walked by him and looked down at the battered girl.

"What the hell is this? What have you done to her?"

"Nothing. She came like that."

The girl was missing a lot of hair. Her forearms were bare. Patches of hair appeared to have been torn out around her head, mostly from the back. She had a couple of bruises, a sizable one on her cheek. Her eyebrows were gone, and in their place, little dots of blood showed where the hair had been torn out.

"Did you give her the bruise on the cheek?"

"No. I knocked her out by the temple."

Denise looked at the girl's wrists. They were raw like someone had tied her up. Duct tape lay balled up on the floor beside her. She fought an internal urge to look away. This had gone too far.

"Tell me again how she came to be here?"

Before the guard could answer, gunfire cut the morning stillness. They both ducked, and then the guard ran for the trailer door.

More gunfire followed. Someone screamed outside.

The battered girl on the floor beside her woke up.

Chapter 36

Things were bad and getting more complicated. He had pulled into the motel and seen an SUV parked at the construction trailer. During the twenty-minute drive to the Sky Blue, he had figured that the trailer would've been the ideal spot for her to stay hidden. And now someone was there.

He had to hide the cruiser before whoever was in the trailer saw him. He steered for the rear of the motel, where, just hours ago, he had dumped the first stolen police car over the hill.

When he got around back, he was greeted by the sight of two large guys in leather jackets standing beside a Cadillac. Right away, he could tell these men were professionals. They stared him down, their hands moving for their inner breast pockets, where Gert assumed their weapons were.

These guys are stupid, he thought. *I'm driving a police car, and they want to draw on me. What the fuck?*

He stopped the car safely out of view of the construction trailer and the highway. Then he opened the door with his left hand and used his right to pull his gun, which he concealed behind his leg.

"Morning, gentlemen. I'll need to see your driver's license and registration."

The guy on the driver's side of the Cadillac turned and looked like he was about to bend into the car while his partner pulled a weapon.

Gert raised his and fired.

A tiny hole formed on the guy's cheek. He didn't get a shot off before he fell to his knees. Then, in slow motion, he collapsed face-first into the dirt.

All this happened in the time it took Gert to turn toward the other guy and fire a second shot. This guy had his gun out in record time. He also had his safety off.

Gert heard the air beside his head part as a bullet passed close by.

It took Gert three shots before he hit the guy in the chest. The driver of the Cadillac got off two, both going wild.

The driver screamed like a girl as he stared down at the blood bubbling from his chest. He fell into the side of his car, dropped to the gravel, and then lay flat. Gert stepped closer and used two more bullets to silence him.

In the aftermath, questions swirled around Gert's head. *I almost bought it here, and for what? Who were these guys?*

He wiped the sweat from his face as he frisked the bodies. No wallets, no identification. Just two guys in a Cadillac, dressed well, who shoot at cops without provocation.

Man, this is fucked up.

Words like *mobsters* and *made men* went through his head. He had never known any, but these guys acted like they were above the law. He realized how lucky he was to still be alive.

Still hunched down by the second man's body, Gert scanned the bushes, his gun leveled in front of him. Then he stared at the windows of the motel.

Nothing. No movement whatsoever.

His heart raced faster now that the gunplay was over. He hadn't been shot at in years. It all started to crash in on him. The morning sun beat down on his back. He should have felt the heat, but he began to shiver. His shirt clung, pasted to him by sweat.

No time to waste pondering. He had to find the girl and get out of the area before more goons showed up.

He headed to the edge of the motel wall, where he peeked around the corner. The SUV was still there.

He tried to find a way to approach the trailer in stealth. From the back appeared to be the best route. The trees came up to the trailer with five feet to spare.

Staying out of the trailer's line of sight, Gert retreated to the woods behind the motel and made his way through them. He crossed a beaten-down path that must have seen better days when the motel was in operation.

Within minutes he was standing behind the construction trailer, using a tree stump to remain unseen.

He reloaded his gun and slipped his finger inside the trigger guard as he walked into the open.

It could be that he had already killed the muscle out by the Cadillac, and he would find no resistance in the trailer. He hoped that was the case.

With the fake police badge in hand, he knocked on the trailer door and stood to one side.

"Police! Open up!"

Chapter 37

AMELIA JUMPED WHEN THE doorbell rang. Caleb, escorted by Detective Johnson, got up to answer it.

"I'm glad you could come, Dolan," Caleb said after opening the door on Sam's cue.

Greetings were made all around while Amelia stood back, feeling wary. Everyone gravitated toward the dining room. She went to the kitchen, where she poured a pot of coffee into an urn. She grabbed the cream and sugar tray and headed to the dining room.

She set the tray down beside the urn and stared at Dolan. Conversation subsided around the table.

"Hello, Mrs. Roberts," Dolan said.

She nodded and was forced to look away. There was something about Dolan's eyes. It felt like he could see into her thoughts. She wondered if mind reading was one of his talents.

She sat in a seat beside Caleb. "I'm happy you're here, especially since you said on the phone that you have an idea where Sarah is, but I still have difficulties with some things."

Caleb placed a hand on Amelia's leg. She read it as a gesture to take it easy and to not forget that Dolan was here to help.

"I know how hard this must be for you," Dolan said. "I'd be happy to clear up any misunderstandings, but we haven't got much time."

"I want my daughter back. That's first and foremost." She forced herself to look at him again. Their eyes locked. Amelia ordered herself not to look away.

"I understand completely," Dolan said. "We're all on the same page. I've worked on several missing persons cases over the years, and thankfully, many of them turned out well. With the information I have, I think we've got a good chance of locating her today. But we need to act soon."

Her head swam. She looked down at her coffee mug. He was saying what she wanted to hear.

"I just need a minute or two. Try to understand something for me. My family visits a psychic fair that you run. One of your *people*," she used her fingers for quotation marks, "meets with my daughter and warns her of danger. We get phone calls from the fair the next day, and then my daughter goes missing, but not before she tries to break into the psychic fairgrounds. A man is dead now, and no one knows where my daughter is. There has got to be more to this fair than I know." She tapped her fingers on the table. "How *is* the fair tied into this?"

"I wouldn't say the fair is tied into it. My people are all intuitive in some way, and if one of them warns a customer about their future, it doesn't make the psychic responsible for that person's well-being. What if you're driving me somewhere, and I notice you're an erratic driver? I say to you if you're going to continue driving like this, one day you'll be in an accident. Then, two days later, you have a car accident. It doesn't make it my fault."

Amelia's eyes glazed over. She decided not to pursue her suspicions this way. "We're all here because you said you knew where my daughter was. If I can get my daughter back, I'm willing to look past several coincidences."

She didn't want to come across as ungrateful, but there was something about Dolan and his psychic fair that she didn't trust.

Dolan shifted in his seat. "I met your daughter at the fair. It was brief, a rather quick meeting, actually. We bumped into each other. She lost her balance and sat on the floor, where she jotted something down in her notebook. Before she stood up, I noticed she had written my name. She'd circled it, and yet we'd never met. Would you know anything about this? You're her parents. Is there anything you can tell me?"

Amelia looked at Caleb for support. He shook his head and said he had no idea how or why Sarah would write Dolan's name in her notebook or circle it.

"When you bumped into Sarah at the fair, why didn't *you* warn her of the danger coming?" Amelia asked.

"I didn't do a reading for her. I don't know everything and everyone.

You have to concentrate and focus while doing a reading. Touch something the person owns, feel the information trickle through my spirit guide."

"But you claim to be psychic?"

"Yes, I do, and I am."

"Then let's get started," Amelia prompted.

Dolan turned to Detective Johnson. "Sam, have you got a tactical team on standby?"

The detective nodded. He had a pen and pad in his hand, waiting to write down whatever Dolan told him.

Caleb reached for the urn that no one else had touched and poured himself a coffee.

"I think Sarah is being held at a cabin on Lake George."

Amelia listened as Dolan gave directions. At one point, he looked at Amelia and Caleb when the detective asked what he would find there. Was Sarah alive? Dolan answered that she was fine, other than some bruising. He said he wasn't getting much more, except they needed to hurry. He felt that her kidnapper was going to move her to a new location or was moving her as they spoke.

Amelia watched everyone spring into action. Detective Johnson got on the phone and started ordering people to the site. Dolan got up and left the room. Other officers made themselves busy with maps.

Caleb looked at her. "I'm going with them," he whispered.

"Me too," she said.

Caleb leaned closer and lowered his voice. "But I think we should follow them in our own car. There's no way they'll let us come along on police business. They'd be worried about the state they find Sarah in."

Amelia nodded. From the corner of her eye, she saw one of the police technicians staring at them. He looked around the room and then beckoned them to join him. Caleb and Amelia got up and followed the tech into Caleb's den.

When they were alone, the cop closed the door behind them.

"I think there's something the two of you should know."

"We want all the information we can get," Caleb said.

"It involves Kim Wepps, a girl who was abducted over seven months ago and then found safe in a farmhouse basement not far from here. The description of her captor resembles witness accounts of the guy who may have kidnapped your daughter on Birk Street. Kim Wepps was taken to an abandoned farm where Dolan *found* her with his psychic powers. I'm not a big believer in psychic stuff, with all these girls kidnapped within six months of each other and by what appears to be the same guy. Just seems a little strange to me."

"What are you saying?" Amelia asked.

"I suspect Dolan is involved in some way."

Amelia and Caleb looked at each other. "Go on," Amelia prodded. "Do your superiors feel the same way?"

"The kidnappings look like they're following a geographical pattern, remaining close to where Dolan is all the time. It just came up recently."

Caleb blinked heavily. "Are you saying Dolan may be masterminding the kidnappings just to be able to locate the victims and look good as a bona fide psychic so his psychic fair can be profitable?"

Amelia could hear the anger in Caleb's voice. She put her hand on his shoulder and rubbed back and forth to calm him.

"We were running through scenarios, working on the kidnapper's MO. In the past five years, we've linked over a dozen kidnappings to the same guy or group. Coincidentally, all of those victims were found by Dolan and his psychic abilities. Kidnappings are happening all over the country, but Dolan only finds the victims of just this one kidnapper with the same MO."

Amelia stepped back and leaned against the wall, taking her hand from Caleb's shoulder. "Does Dolan know that you guys suspect him?"

"Not yet. Detective Johnson doesn't want him to know anything until Sarah is brought home. Whether Dolan is involved in a crime or he's really psychic doesn't matter as long as Sarah's still out there. If we tip Dolan off, things could go south. But if Dolan is kept in the dark, Sarah will come home safe like all the other victims before her, and then we can work on Dolan."

"Okay then, let's go," Caleb said.

"Where're you going?" the cop asked.

"To Lake George to get our daughter."

Chapter 38

Gert took a deep breath, steadied himself, then knocked on the trailer again. Rustling sounds came from inside. Someone was definitely there.

He checked behind him. Nothing moved except the natural foliage flow in the gentle morning breeze cruising through the area. Even the highway was quiet.

More sounds came to him from behind the door. He leaned closer, almost touching the wood with his ear. It sounded like two people were arguing in a whisper.

He knocked on the door with the butt of the gun. "Police! Open up!"

The lock clicked. Gert stepped back, his gun raised.

The door opened, and a woman stepped into view.

"Come out slowly, with your hands up. Is there anyone else in there with you?" He winked one eye, batting at a drop of sweat.

"I need to see a badge," the woman said. "I heard shots, and now I'm being ordered out of the trailer at gunpoint. You don't look like a cop."

Gert knew a gun could be trained on him at that moment. He needed to play this cool.

What the hell is this place?

If security was tight enough to use goons like the two dead guys in the back, then these people were being extra cautious for a reason. He lowered his gun in a friendly gesture.

"I'm spooked, too, ma'am. I drove around back for a routine visit to these premises and got shot at. I have backup on the way. An officer went missing sometime last night. Witnesses reported seeing his patrol car heading out of town in this direction. We're checking everything out."

Gert loved it when he thought quickly. The trailer was here yesterday, so it was safe to assume someone might have seen him dump the cop car.

He lifted his fake badge high enough for the woman to see. She leaned forward and squinted in the sun. Only an expert would be able to tell his badge was a fake.

The woman stepped from the trailer. "Is it okay if I keep my hands at my side? I'm not armed."

Gert nodded. "Just no sudden movements. Who are you, and why are you here? What is this place?"

"My name is Denise Hall. I own this property. I'm planning to renovate the motel and then sell it."

"So, why the two goons in the back? Why would they start shooting at a cop without provocation?" He was surprised at how official-like he sounded.

She moved away from him, her head lowered like she was thinking of an appropriate response.

Then a cell phone rang from somewhere.

"Do you mind if I take this call?" she asked.

He felt it would look suspicious if he said no. "Go ahead."

He watched her slowly pull out a cell phone. She flipped it open and said hello.

He took the opportunity to scan the area.

When he turned back to her, she had a strange look on her face. He couldn't quite read it.

She told the person on the other end of the line that she would call them back and then flipped her phone shut.

"Everything okay?" he asked. "You look like you've seen a ghost."

"That was my mother." The woman looked back at her cell phone in wonderment. "After over twenty years, she calls me with a warning."

Her face lost all color. The woman started shaking her head. She took a few small steps away from him toward the open parking lot.

Something was wrong. Something he didn't understand.

He adjusted his grip on the gun handle where sweat had cooled his palm. At any moment, he might have to drop and shoot.

"Why did you knock on the trailer door?" she asked.

What an odd question. She must be pretty stupid. "If you had people shoot at you for no reason, you'd check the area out, too."

"Right. But why not wait for backup? Who knows how many people could be in the trailer or how heavily armed they could be."

She continued to move around until she was on the highway side of him. Now he stood with his back to the trailer. He wasn't an idiot. Someone else was in the trailer, and he figured it was the girl.

The woman stared at him.

He had run out of time. She was stalling.

He raised his gun, fired, and jumped to the right, all in one motion. His bullet missed the woman.

This was not exactly something he practiced, but it made him feel like he was in the movies.

The ground was hard, winding him when he landed on his right shoulder. The landing didn't quite go as planned.

Dust plumed up in a small torrent about his face. Someone was shooting at him now. Small explosions erupted inches away.

He rolled toward the trailer. Within seconds he was under the shelter of the trailer's wooden steps.

The woman was running past the SUV parked in the lot. She was going for the highway. He aimed and fired three quick shots. He saw at least one hit her.

She fell and grabbed her lower right leg. Her wails reached him with unnerving accuracy. Gert knew he wouldn't be able to hear anyone in the trailer now.

He turned and crawled deeper under it, constantly scanning the area around him for legs to appear from the trailer.

Dust filled his nose. Breathing became a chore when he stopped crawling and rolled onto his back. He braced his elbows in the dirt, edged out from under the trailer, and looked up the side. A solitary window sat directly above him.

The woman continued to scream in the dirt. He felt it resonate through his body with a kind of joy.

He squirmed forward, clearing the edge of the trailer. There were only a couple of bullets left in his weapon. He would have to do this right the first time.

He stood and peeked around the edge to look at the main door.

No one was visible. The shooter was still inside.

He took a large step toward the door and threw his badge inside the trailer. While the badge was still in flight, he ran back to the window at the end of the trailer.

He popped his head up and looked in. A large man stood staring at the door with a gun strapped to his shoulder.

Gert put his gun to the screen side of the window. He aimed as best he could and fired all the remaining ammunition into the trailer.

After the noise of gunfire faded, the area had an eerie quiet to it. The woman in the motel parking lot only muttered to herself now, her screaming abated.

He ducked down and scurried around the back, where he came to another window. He eased up and looked in. The big guy lay on the floor with his hands clamped around his neck. Blood gushed through his fingers.

Gert was surprised at how little he felt when snuffing a life out. There had been too much killing, and he was growing numb to it.

The sun beat down on his back. He agreed with it. This place was hot. It was time to go before people started showing up.

He ran around to the front and up the stairs. His gun was empty, but he kept it raised in a firing position as he entered the trailer.

The big guy wasn't moving now as blood circled his head.

Gert searched the trailer, end to end. This was his last chance. He had to find the girl and leave.

He encountered a wall built to block this part of the trailer from the rest. He kicked the door five times before it buckled and broke open.

And there was his prize. His little *automatic writer*. He aimed the gun at her, grabbed her by the wrist, and started for the door.

She whimpered and shook her head, appearing dazed.

A new plan formed when he stepped outside. The SUV would be a much better vehicle than the cop car. He opened the back door of the SUV and pushed the girl inside without too much resistance. She was acting lethargic, cradling her head in her hands.

He looked at the steering column. No keys.

The woman on the ground lay sprawled out, sweating and pale, her eyes wide. Blood circled her lower leg and foot.

"Keys," he said, waving his hand in the air. "Give them to me, and I won't kill you."

She pointed at the left pocket of her slacks. He bent and fished inside, where he found the keys.

"Good. You tell them the truth about what happened here. Tell everyone who asks that I've got the girl, and I will kill her if I don't get what I want."

Gert turned to leave and then stopped. There had been so many things wrong with this from the start. There was no way he could return to living a normal life of small-time jobs.

After the cop was killed on the highway, Gert knew his boss was lying to him. There would be no other city, no other kidnappings.

The team was dead.

His boss would want him dead because if he was captured, he could finger every last member of the team.

He knew it was over.

He turned and looked down at the woman in the dirt. The blood had slowed its exit from her ankle area. She had been applying constant pressure, trying to staunch the flow. He noticed the sun glint off something in her hand. Her cell phone.

Good. She probably called for help.

"Whatever you say to the cops will be heard by the man I work for. Tell them that I've decided I will finish this my way."

Chapter 39

Sam looked through the windshield of the unmarked cruiser at the passing clouds. Some were dark with rain, others gray and dreary.

"I wonder if the weather's gonna hold off," Sam said.

Dolan didn't answer him. They'd been on the side of the highway for ten minutes, waiting for Sergeant McKinley's Emergency Task Force to give them the go-ahead to approach the cabin.

"You okay, Dolan?"

"Sure."

"You seem tense. Something you want to talk about?"

Dolan shook his head. "I'm a little confused on this one. There's something different about this case."

"How's that?" Sam grabbed his coffee from the holder in the dash and took a sip.

"I don't know much yet, but it's coming to me."

"What *do* you know?"

Dolan looked at him. Sam set his coffee back. "I know someone close to me is going to get killed."

"Close to you emotionally or in proximity? I mean, I'm sitting right beside you. That would suck …" He smiled and then asked, "What if we get this guy right now? He's supposed to be in the cabin, right?"

"When I first mentioned the cabin, I said we had to work fast because the perp was planning to leave or was leaving at that very moment."

"Are you saying he's gone?"

"Yes, I think so."

"Why would certain information be blocked from you, but other snippets come through? Don't you usually get enough of the picture to be more than fifty percent, right?"

"Usually, but I'm being blocked this time."

"Blocked? How does that happen? And who would block you? Or better yet, who would have the talent to know how?"

Dolan shrugged like he had just lost a baseball game. *Oh well, no big deal*, his expression said.

Well, it is a big deal, Sam thought.

Someone whistled outside. He looked up as one of McKinley's men waved them in.

Sam turned the car on and drove down a gravel road until he took the left-hand turn onto the cabin's private drive. He parked, and the two of them got out.

McKinley walked up to him. "Sam, we're too late. Looks like they were here recently, though. Come inside. I'll show you what we've got."

Sam nodded and looked at Dolan. He was staring off at the trees. Sam followed Dolan's gaze and saw nothing there. A soft rain started to patter down around them.

"You coming in?" he asked.

Dolan shook his head. "Just get it over with. I've got some thinking to do."

***

Dolan stood under a tall pine tree, watching McKinley's men come and go from the cabin.

Maybe everything seemed different this time because the person he was trying to locate also had a psychic talent. Could it work like repelling magnets?

He didn't want his colleagues to think he could not produce results. He knew, however, there would be signs in the cabin to show that Sarah had been there. Signs that would vindicate him as a psychic.

He stepped out from under the pine tree and into the light rain. The air held a faint wet-wood smell, making him think of the Sky Blue Motel.

He stopped halfway to the cabin. *Sky Blue?* He looked up. Rain came from darkened clouds with no *blue sky* anywhere. *Motel?*

Where did that come from?

He trudged up the steps of the cabin. The kitchen area held minor details of residency. Utensils in disarray, scraps, and crumbs on the countertop, chairs left astride the table.

He could hear McKinley talking about Sarah in one of the back rooms. He headed that way and peeked in. The men were standing by a small desk with books scattered on it.

McKinley turned to him. "It looks like you are good at what you do. Fingerprints in this room, at first glance, appear to be Sarah's. We'll have confirmation shortly. Now, if you could just lead us to where she *is* and not where she *was*."

Dolan nodded at him, turned around, and walked out of the cabin. The rain had subsided to a gentle mist. A soft breeze moved through the trees, causing them to serenade him with a billowing hum of leaves.

Someone shouted. It looked like McKinley's men had stopped a car from entering the cabin's driveway.

He recognized Caleb's voice.

What's he doing here?

Was Amelia with him? Dolan would have to deal with this. They would want to know where their daughter was. Why was she not where he said she would be? Was she still okay? It would all boil down to one thing. Was there still any hope?

He hurried up to the road. Sarah's father was standing by his car, animated in his frustration at being denied access to the cabin.

Caleb saw him and called him over.

"Did you find Sarah?" Caleb asked. "Is she okay?"

His face looked desperate. Since Caleb hadn't seen his daughter yet and he was being denied access to the premises, Dolan figured Caleb was thinking the worst.

"She's gone. We missed her. I'm sorry."

Caleb gasped. A small yip came from inside the car.

Dolan realized his mistake by saying *she was gone.*

"I mean, she's not here. There is evidence that she was here, but we're too late."

Caleb frowned, holding the open door of his car with both hands. "So she's ... whoever was here has left the area?"

"Yes."

"I thought you'd done this before. I thought you were the best. What went wrong?"

"Nothing went wrong. The information isn't accurate all the time. I'm not a fax machine. I don't receive a detailed list, and we all follow the instructions. Only God knows everything." He realized his tone was harsher than he intended, but everyone needed to step back.

"What are you talking about? Either you see things, or you don't. These are people's *lives* you're dealing with. You can't send everyone on wild goose chases."

"It's not that simple," Dolan said. "I wish it were, but it's not. She was here, but she isn't now."

The officer guarding the access road to the cabin stepped between Dolan and Caleb. He told Caleb he would have to clear the road. Get back in his car and move it to the highway.

Caleb mumbled under his breath and leaned down to get in his car. He put it in gear and started to back out.

Dolan turned toward the cabin to see Sam coming out the front door. He was talking on his cell phone. A moment later, he flipped it shut and beckoned Dolan over.

As Dolan approached, Sam started talking. "A woman named Denise Hall is being rushed to Liberty Memorial Hospital with a gunshot wound to her ankle. Emergency crews found her alive along with three dead bodies at an abandoned motel called the Sky Blue."

Dolan stared at him. *Sky Blue Motel.*

"What's up? You look surprised."

Dolan realized his mouth was open. "I'm not used to having information given to me this way."

"What way?" Sam mocked exaggeration.

"The name of the motel came to me five minutes ago, but that's all I got. Nothing else. Now you come up and tell me things I should've known. It seems to be happening too fast."

Sam flipped open a notebook and scanned down the page. "Apparently, she owns the motel and had recently renovated it. The three dead men were security, although they were heavily armed, and two of the dead may be attached to the Ward family. The bad news is yet to come."

Dolan nodded for Sam to go on.

"It looks like the FBI has an interest in the Ward family. One of the two dead was an informant. He was one of theirs. And get this. Denise says a teenage girl with missing hair was taken by the guy who shot her ankle."

Dolan was struck with a thought. "What was the woman's name again?"

"Denise Hall."

Dolan snapped his fingers. "That's Esmerelda's daughter. Sarah said something to Mary Bennett about Esmerelda's daughter. Something about her getting shot. So she *is* psychic." He said this last part to himself.

"Here's why they called us. They found a cop car at the back of the motel. It was stolen earlier in the morning. Local police knew that we were looking for the guy who killed the cop on the side of the highway and stole *his* car, too. They wanted to give us the heads up. But they also had a message from this woman, Denise. She said the perp told her to tell the police that he would finish things his way now. She also said the guy told her that whatever she tells the police, his boss would hear it, too."

Dolan watched Sam as he wiped the edge of his mouth twice. He looked disturbed, bothered.

"What's got me is the message from the kidnapper. If his boss hears whatever Denise tells the cops, then that would lead us to believe that his boss is in our ranks. The media is concentrating on the cop-killer case. There hasn't been a media frenzy on Sarah's kidnapping, so the only people who would be privy to Denise's comments would be everyone working directly on the kidnapping of Sarah Roberts. I'm also concerned about the dead informant, not to mention the Ward family connection. This case is rapidly becoming something much bigger than I anticipated. The FBI may want to get involved now."

Dolan thought about Esmerelda. He heard Sam's cell phone ring. Sam stepped away from him to get out of the rain.

Dolan walked over to a large pine to find a moment's shelter.

The whole time he felt Sam's eyes on him. Things were going wrong fast, and now everyone on this case was going to be suspicious of each other.

Dolan wondered how he would get out of this mess and keep his hands clean.

Chapter 40

SARAH OPENED HER EYES and then snapped them shut. She massaged her temples. Heat from the sun bathed her skin. It made her think she was lying in the desert.

Through half-closed eyes, she could see her only company was garbage. A gentle breeze pushed a newspaper past chunks of broken glass. Candy wrappers littered an area that looked like a trash bag had been upturned.

She managed to get her eyes open past slits, even as the heat from the sun hammered at her head.

She was in what looked like a rundown building that appeared to be abandoned. The windows were gaping holes where the glass used to be. Graffiti covered the walls.

She moved her legs back and forth and was glad to find them free, untied. Only her left wrist was tied, with some leather straps bolted together. She rolled onto her back and closed her eyes as the sun hit her face.

When she tugged on her left wrist, it caught at the end of its tether in midair. The leather strap was tied with rope to a pipe protracted from the wall. She tugged again and watched the pipe shift where it was connected to her leash. She yanked harder, causing the pipe to shake more, bits of the wall falling loose.

She was alone. Her head still pounded, but some things were more important.

In a sitting position, she used both hands to yank on the strap. More drywall crumbled away, but the pipe stood firm. Coiled as it was, she found it too difficult to pry off in her weakened state. A smaller lock kept the leather strap secured to her wrist.

Her stomach tightened with hunger pains so strong she felt nauseous. Her tongue moved from side to side, sticking to the inner edges of her mouth.

With both feet braced against the wall, she yanked again, using resources she didn't know she still had.

It was not enough to break free.

The pipe remained fixed to something behind the wall.

The cooling breeze from the nearest window moved across her face. She heard footsteps. Someone was coming. She turned around and leaned back against the wall.

"You're awake."

Her captor walked over and set two water bottles by her feet. She lunged for one, unscrewed the white cap, and guzzled almost half the bottle, spilling some down her chin. The water was cool. She felt it hit her stomach and enjoyed the cold feeling in her throat.

She touched the back of her neck, where she found hair. A feeling of ease came over her.

I can handle this.

She hadn't gotten away, but she could handle this. Everything was right back where they'd left off at the motel when she'd given him the slip.

She wondered if her stomach would ever be the same. That nervous pang, the constant butterflies. She wondered if she could get an ulcer from prolonged nervousness.

"This will all be over within days."

Does that mean he's gonna let me go?

She doubted it.

He sat across from her. "Do you fear death?"

She picked up the water bottle and drank from it again, ignoring him. She didn't know when she'd get another chance. Her fingers seized and pulled hard on the hair nestled in the most sensitive spot at the top of her neck.

"Why are you pulling your hair?"

She remained quiet. Gert shrugged and leaned back on his outstretched arms.

"I'm surprised you haven't broken yet. I guess some girls take longer than others. Some things are scarier than just losing your life, you know."

Sarah watched him from the corner of her eye.

"I've decided I need to kill someone from your family."

She jerked her head around, causing her headache to flare.

"Oh, now I've got your attention." He smirked.

She wondered if he was serious or just playing with her. He'd already done so much damage to her family. She was sure her mother was worried about her, and her father was probably losing his mind trying to figure out what to do.

"I think I'll execute your mother. Then we'll be even. I'll use a car to run her down in the road as you did to my brother. What do you think? Would that be fair?"

"You can't be serious," she said, her hand tightening on the water bottle. Her voice surprised her with its grating quality.

"After you're dead, I will kill your mother." He did an exaggerated nod of his head, his eyes psycho-wide. She could see the craziness behind his eyes.

Sarah used all the leverage she had to swing the water bottle. It made perfect contact with his cheek before bouncing off and sliding away on the floor.

She got in a defensive stance. Her breath came out in pants, matching the throbbing in her head.

"You think you're tough?" he asked. "Is that it?"

He got his feet under him and stood. She eased back against the wall as he walked away. He pulled out his cell phone and held it up. It looked like he was checking for signal strength.

"I'm waiting for a call. In the meantime, let me tell you about murder." He turned back to her. "Everyone who dies is making room for the rest of us. Humans are at the top of the food chain. We aren't hunted by anything or anyone other than ourselves. We're our own predators. If people had only died from old age, the world would've been overpopulated long ago. That's what murder does. That's why we had World War One and World War Two. Population control."

Sarah slid back down and sat against the wall. She opened the other water bottle and drank from it. She tuned him out as he walked to different parts of the room, looking at his cell phone.

She wondered what her parents were doing right now. Were they working with the police to find her? Would it be the police who rescued her?

She didn't have much faith in that, especially after what this guy told the woman, who Sarah guessed was Esmerelda's daughter when he stole her SUV at the motel. It was looking more and more like she would have to get out of this on her own.

"Believe it or not, I'm doing something for the greater good when I kill people," Gert continued. "Trust me when I say I will kill you, and the world will be a better place for it."

He frowned, rubbed an eyebrow, and turned in a half circle. He lifted his arm, checked the watch on his wrist, and then swore to himself. Then he grunted, scratched his cheek, and frowned again, making him look absolutely insane.

A moment later, he rounded the corner at the end of the room and left her alone.

She grabbed the rope and pulled with renewed enthusiasm.

***

Gert hit redial and put the phone to his ear. It rang three times before his employer picked it up.

"What's up?" the boss asked.

"Tell me how close the police are. What's my next move?"

"There is no *next move*. You've gone too far this time. You're on your own. And don't call me again."

"Wait! What're you talking about?"

"How many people have we killed in the years you, your brother, and I have been doing this?"

"I don't know. Maybe two?"

"Right. As a practice, we let them all go, yet you killed three more people at the motel, not to mention the cop you almost killed when you hit him in the throat. That would've been two cops dead. As it stands, it looks like they'll be organizing some kind of manhunt. I think the FBI will be getting involved soon. This is the kind of thing you escape by leaving the *fucking* country."

Gert listened while he leaned against a wall. He turned toward it and tapped his forehead back and forth against the chipped paint.

"My advice is to find out what this girl can do psychically and then see if you can use it to your advantage. You should keep her alive until you get somewhere safe. They won't hesitate to shoot you if you're alone, but everyone will be more cautious if they know you have the girl. That's all I can offer you."

Gert's forehead hurt, but he kept it up, repeatedly tapping into the wall.

"Are you banging your head against the wall again?"

"Yes."

"Why do you do that?"

"Because I like the feeling when I stop."

"You're fucked. I'm hanging up and destroying this cell phone. You will never be able to reach me again. Don't forget; no one will believe you when you tell them I was involved."

"I've got proof of your involvement. I go down, you go down, too," Gert flipped his phone shut.

He moved away from the wall. He had to think. There was always a way out. He could choose death by cop. Kill as many as he could get before they took him. That meant he could see his brother again. He was sure that after death, his brother would be there waiting wherever he was going.

But what was he going to do about the girl? He cursed under his breath. Now he was getting angry. Had she not meddled in their affairs, everything would be fine. His brother would still be alive.

He realized more than ever that this situation was past saving. There would be no going back to the old way of life. It was time to start thinking about what country he would live in. Mexico, Cuba, somewhere in South America, Europe? An image of Sarah splayed out, blood all over her, while he put the gun under his own chin came to mind. He could just go and kill her right now and then himself. Simple solution.

He shook his head. *That would be a last resort.*

The public never really knew how many unsolved murders and missing persons were out there. He was pretty safe as long as he was not arrested for anything or fingerprinted.

Although, the police will never stop looking for a cop killer.

He headed to the SUV for a pen and paper. A minute later, he returned to the room that housed his prisoner.

She had been busy. The pipe she was attached to sat askew, bent, and sticking halfway out of the wall.

"Write something," he said, tossing the implements at her.

He used a key from his pocket to undo the lock on her leather strap. It took him a long, frustrating minute maneuvering the rope to get it all undone.

Sarah looked up at him. "What happened to your forehead?"

"Write something!" he shouted.

She jumped back, startled by his shout. Fumbling with the pad, she opened it and got her pen ready.

"What do you want me to write?" she whispered.

"Whatever your informer tells you to write."

"It doesn't work like that," she said.

"Today it does."

Gert lunged forward and grabbed her neck. He tightened his grip enough to close her windpipe. She slumped down, gasping for air. She was trying to speak, but nothing came out.

"What'd you say?" he asked.

He released her enough to talk.

"Only … when I … blackout … can I get a … message …"

"I can help that along."

He let go of her neck and yanked his gun from his waistband.

"No," she stammered. "Not knocked unconscious. Involuntary blackouts." She struggled to sit upright, holding her neck. He forced her back down.

"The blackouts come and go," she continued. "Sometimes once a week, sometimes more. I never know when until I look in my notebook and see a message there. If you let me keep this pen and paper, I'll be able to write something when the next blackout comes."

"I'm not going to give you much time." He stood and scanned the room. "Make me happy, Sarah. I'm not fun to be around when I'm angry."

Most people escape their nightmares by waking up.

Sarah escaped hers by going to sleep.

Chapter 41

Dolan sat quietly as Sam pulled the car up alongside Sarah's parents. Caleb rolled his window down.

"You guys hanging in?" Sam asked.

"I don't want to give you a hard time, Detective," Caleb said. "We just want our daughter back. I appreciate, Dolan," he said, averting his eyes around Sam, "that you've joined the investigation. I guess we thought this would come together quicker than it has. I mean, I've heard about some of your successes, Mr. Ryan. It's just hard for us not to see Sarah here."

Dolan nodded. He caught a glimpse of Amelia wiping her face.

"We probably put too much stock in Dolan coming up with this location so fast," Caleb added.

Dolan flashed back to the note he had found while wandering the Roberts's house, looking for something to attach himself to, something to cue his gift into action. When he touched things in Sarah's bedroom, he came across an envelope under her pillow. He had pulled it out and seen his name on the outside. It wasn't sealed. He had opened it and pulled the paper out from within.

The letter had been from Sarah. She said she knew something dangerous was working toward her, but it was unavoidable. She had to try to stop a kidnapping. She told him she had no choice because of her conscience. Sarah felt she would make it out okay because the one who writes through her wouldn't send her to die after all the good she had done.

Dolan had folded the note up, intending to share it with everyone, but it had been forgotten in the rush to leave for Lake George. He figured now wasn't the best time to bring it up, especially with people putting less faith in him.

"We're all doing our best," Sam said. "We will catch this guy. We're on our way to talk to a woman who saw your daughter and her kidnapper just a few hours ago. We've got a description and which direction they were headed in. We also know the vehicle and plate number the perp is driving. Hang in there. This may come together faster than you think."

Caleb looked at his wife and then back at Sam. "We're following you to this woman."

"I can't let you do that. I'd lose my badge."

Dolan read the persistence on Caleb's face.

"If this woman was the last known person to see my daughter, then Amelia and I want to talk to her, too."

"Well, you can't come with us, but it's a free country. I wouldn't be able to stop you if you were to go to Liberty Memorial hospital to see a woman named Denise Hall. That's up to you."

Sam dropped the cruiser into gear and pulled away. The rain had subsided before they had left the cabin, but the road was still wet. Sam flipped the wipers on as they came up behind a tractor-trailer.

"Is Sarah gonna make it, Dolan?" Sam asked.

"Can't tell for certain."

"What *can* you tell for certain?"

Dolan detected an edge of hostility in Sam's voice.

He was saved from answering by the ring of his cell phone. It was Alex, his assistant. Dolan updated him on the situation and when he was likely to get back to the fair.

If not today, this would probably be over by tomorrow, he told him.

Chapter 42

With the small amount of light from the dash, Sarah leaned forward and read the note in her hand. She had no idea when the blackout had come, but it clearly had happened while she was sleeping. As she read the messages, she found two things unsettling and peculiar.

After months of getting cryptic messages about people in peril, she had never expected them to get personal.

This message from the Other Side was the most serious one yet.

Sarah sat in the back seat of the SUV. They had been traveling all day. The sun had already gone down. He had pulled over to grab food and let her pee in the bushes.

She'd been asleep for a while, and now, when she looked over the seat, the clock on the dash read after one in the morning.

Her captor seemed to be talking to himself, although she could not determine what he was saying. She was becoming more worried as his actions grew increasingly harried. He appeared to be coming undone, completely losing touch with reality.

Sarah looked away and tried to focus on the note.

Could this be a test? Maybe she was being promoted to handle bigger and more serious tasks when this was all over. That thought offered hope. It would mean she was destined to get out of her predicament alive. Why would the message giver not tell her how things were supposed to be? It was unfair to play with her like this. How much trauma could one depression-prone person take?

Sarah read the note again. It came in three parts, with some of it fading away.

Don't thump, rip, and tear, better to be savage.

Gert's boss will kill him.

Gert's boss works with polic.

The *c* was half written, and the *e* on *police* was missing.

Sarah considered how much of it she wanted Gert to see. She knew she had to show him something, though.

What if he thought she had made it up to undermine him?

It would be better to show him all of it so he could see the mystery of the first riddle. Maybe seen as a package, it would lend more credence to the message.

On the back of the paper, she noticed a girl's name: *Vivian Roberts.*

Who the hell is Vivian Roberts?

This was the first message Sarah had written out that pertained to the here and now. One that actually related to the situation she was facing. It coincided with Gert's demands. He had ordered something written, and now he would get it.

What if all of the messages were her subconscious telling her stuff she already knew?

She dismissed the idea a second later. How could she know where to be when people were in trouble? How could she have known to bring a hammer that day at the river? She could be psychic and in the infancy of her gift, but she didn't think that was the case.

She recalled reading somewhere that sleepwalkers could open doors, drive cars, and even commit murder while remaining asleep. People had used somnambulism as a defense in court and won.

Could she be writing notes in her sleep?

She brought her legs up under her and hugged them. The temperature was cool, but a sheen of sweat covered her body.

She had to get away from Gert.

She would have to rely on the Other Side for directions or handle it herself.

She just hoped she wouldn't have to kill again.

Chapter 43

Amelia thought the house looked different as they approached. Something about it at night made it look sad.

Caleb parked, turned off the car, and sat back.

It had been an exhausting day. When they finally got to talk to Denise Hall, she was being sedated for the pain. The relentless interview schedule with different police agencies had worn her out. Amelia and Caleb only got a minute out of Denise before she fell into a drug-induced sleep. In that minute, they learned that Sarah had looked tired but was otherwise okay.

Amelia got out of the car. Caleb did the same, and they entered their house, which didn't feel like their home anymore. It felt foreign, with the police officers milling around, sipping coffee.

Despite how many people were there, the house felt empty, too.

Amelia stepped away from Caleb. "I need to be alone for a while."

He nodded and turned for the kitchen.

She took the stairs slowly like her soul was burdened by the weight of grief. Amelia flopped on the bed when she entered her bedroom and looked up at the ceiling. She felt helpless and exhausted. There was nothing she could do but wait. It was beginning to drive her crazy.

She got up and walked into the bathroom. The mirror reminded her she hadn't applied makeup since the morning of the psychic fair. The weight of the unknown had aged her in the two short days Sarah had been gone.

She left the bathroom a moment later, only to collapse on the bed again, tears streaming down her cheeks. She wondered how she could stand to lose another child.

I would certainly become a different person, she thought. *One very closed off from the world.*

This was the second time a daughter of hers had been kidnapped. She would do whatever was necessary to ensure this wouldn't be the second time a daughter of hers was killed.

She fell asleep crying over the loss of Sarah and the chaos her life had become. She wept because she couldn't put it back together again.

Chapter 44

CALEB WALKED THROUGH THE main floor of the house and stopped in the kitchen, where he grabbed a glass and opened a bottle of brandy. After two quick shots, he left the kitchen and approached the stereo in the living room. He tuned it to the local rock station and turned up the volume. Not loud enough to bother anyone but high enough to drown out what he wanted to do. He didn't want Amelia to hear anything.

An officer stood beside a temporary workstation set up by the kitchen phone line, flipping pages back and forth on a clipboard.

"I need answers," Caleb said. "I need to know what we're doing here. I don't want to be told that we're sitting on our *fucking* asses waiting for a kidnapper to call."

Caleb figured these guys deal with angry people for a living. Caleb was just another upset father.

"We're hoping to intercept a call. In cases like this, we usually get a call with a list of demands."

"'*Most times*,'" Caleb mocked. "This isn't *most times* because there's been no call. There are no demands. So why don't you all just leave."

The officer set his clipboard down on the table behind him. "It would be better if we stayed. Things would go downhill fast if we were to leave and then miss the call that saves your daughter."

"I understand that you guys are the experts and that you've done all this before, but it's different this time. He's got my daughter and out there killing people."

"Every cop in the country is looking for him now. He shot one of ours.

He raised the stakes, so there would be no way we could abandon this post knowing that the one person he has with him lives here."

Caleb didn't want to hear anything more the cop was saying, but he couldn't stop talking. "What about Dolan? I thought he could help. I practically begged—"

A knock on the front door silenced him. He spun and started for it, but the cop grabbed his arm.

"You aren't expecting anyone, are you?"

Caleb mouthed the word *no*. They started for the door together, with the officer putting himself against the wall behind it.

Caleb stood a little off-center. "Who is it?" he shouted.

"FBI."

The cop reached past Caleb and looked through the small window beside the door. Then he unlocked and opened it.

Caleb watched as they showed identification and stepped in.

"My name is Special Agent Jill Hanover, and this is my partner, Special Agent Fergus Mant. We're in charge now," she said to the cop. "Your task force is being dismantled. Everyone can pack up and leave. I'll have my own people handle things from here."

Chapter 45

Sam jolted awake. Something had awakened him, but he wasn't sure what.

His cell phone rang.

That had to be it.

He fumbled in the dark, trying to remember where he'd placed it in the shoddy motel room.

His hand found the light switch of the bedside lamp on the third ring. The phone was on the floor. He bent over, snatched it up, and flipped it open in one movement.

"Detective Sam Johnson here."

"It's Mike. We've got a problem."

"What's the problem?"

"We're dismantling our equipment and leaving the Roberts's house."

Sam was wide awake now. "Why are you doing that?" He swung his legs off the bed and sat up.

"FBI is taking over the case."

"I *am* the FBI. The FBI commissioned the task force. This can't be happening."

"It is. You had better get here fast before this Roberts guy gets arrested. He wants everyone out. The Special Agent in charge is trying to calm him down."

Sam raised his free hand to his forehead. Why was the FBI sending a team to take over a kidnapping case from the multi-jurisdictional task force set up to handle kidnapping cases?

"I'm on my way."

Sam slammed his phone on the bed and looked at the door between his and Dolan's room. It had to be Dolan. Whatever the problem was, he was sure Dolan was at the root of it.

He knew there was something different about this case. And he knew that difference lay with Dolan.

He stood, stretched, and walked over to the door. He heard nothing coming from Dolan's room. His hand was in midair, about to knock, when the door unlocked and flipped open from the other side.

"I'm ready to go," Dolan said.

"It's four-thirty in the morning," Sam said. "I thought you'd be sleeping."

"I was, but when I found out the FBI was taking the case from you, I got up and dressed."

"How did you find out?"

"Come on, Sam, how long have we been doing this? You know I have my ways."

Dolan stepped away from the door and grabbed his duffel bag. He called over his shoulder to meet him in the coffee shop in the lobby when Sam was ready.

Sam shut the adjoining door and started getting dressed, thinking about the questions Dolan would have to answer soon.

<h1 style="text-align:center">Chapter 46</h1>

SSARAH FELT HER WRISTS being tugged, then they dropped apart, free of restraint. She rolled her head to the side and got her eyes open enough to guess the time as early morning. The sun was up, and the air was cool. Birds flitted past the open windows of the building she sat in.

How many days had it been? How long before it was all over? She couldn't continue this way. She was the one in charge usually. She was the one helping people, not the person who needed the help. She wondered if her message giver knew what would happen to her when Sarah was sent to stop the kidnapping on Birk Street.

Instead of stopping the kidnapping from taking place, maybe she was supposed to be taken so her actions would get these guys caught.

That may not have been the case because people had been killed. The message giver from the Other Side wouldn't have sent her into this knowing so many lives were in danger.

A hand wrapped around her arm and lifted her. She was surprised by his strength and equally aware of the loss of power in her legs. She could barely hold herself up. Pain shot from her ankles. She looked at her feet as they hustled along but lost her balance and fell head-first to the dirty wooden floor.

He yanked her up and started her walking again. They went down a flight of stairs, around a corner, and out of the building through an old loading dock.

A black van sat idling, its side door gaping. He pushed her in the back and slammed the door shut. Sarah leaned up on an elbow and massaged her right wrist. The driver's side door opened, and Gert got in.

Within minutes they were on the highway. A small wooden bench stretched along the backdoor of the van. She edged over and sat up on it.

He had not restrained her. Sarah was sure he didn't just forget. It was probably because she was zapped of any energy, and he wasn't afraid of her running.

"I saw what you wrote," he said.

She could see him watching her from the rearview mirror. She looked away, not sure how to respond yet. The last day or so was a blur. She was in a building, then an SUV, and then another building. It worried her to be so out of it, although it made sense because she hadn't eaten in at least three days.

"You were right, by the way," he added.

"About what?" Sarah asked.

"My boss does work with the police. Thank you for the inside tip about him wanting to kill me. I should tell you, though, I already figured that out myself."

Sarah could see that the message had calmed him. He almost looked happy today.

"That's why you're not tied up right now. I want your hands free to write if you go into another trance. Anything else you want to write for me would be useful. Like, how can I get out of this mess? I will reward you kindly."

"You don't need me for that. Let me go and run for Mexico. You might make it. That's how you get out of this mess."

"Cute."

Gert drove down an exit ramp and pulled up to a red light. He turned and faced her. "The only reason I'm talking to you is because of your talent. I've provided a pen and paper by the bench there." He pointed to her left. "Write as much as possible in the time we have left together. Maybe something will be useful to me."

Sarah picked up the paper and pen. She opened the notepad and flipped through a few of the wire-bound pages.

The light had changed to green. Gert spun back around in his seat and started the van going again.

"If you try any funny business of any kind, you know what'll happen to you. This isn't over yet, and we're not friends. Are we clear?"

"Yes," Sarah whispered.

She thought about a plan. She had to get the circulation in her hands and legs going so she could run.

She thought about Dolan. She had left a note for him. Could he be the guy that was Gert's boss? After all, the message said Gert's boss works with the police. It didn't say the boss was a cop. Who else works with the police?

And how did he learn about my automatic writing abilities unless he talked to Dolan or Esmerelda?

The familiar stirrings in her vision and the numbness in her left arm warned her of a blackout.

She slid to the van's floor and grabbed the pen just as she lost consciousness.

Chapter 47

FBI-ISSUED VEHICLES LITTERED the front of the Roberts's house as Sam and Dolan pulled into the driveway. The sun was rising. The dash clock said it was just after six in the morning.

Sam looked over at Dolan, who had what seemed to be a resigned look on his face. They hadn't talked much on the way from the motel. Both just sat there, watching the sky get lighter and brighter the closer they got to the Roberts's house.

At the front door, someone pulled a curtain back. Then the door opened.

A woman stepped onto the front porch with her hand out to shake.

"I'm Special Agent Jill Hanover. You must be Detective Sam Johnson."

Hands were shaken, and introductions were made. They all stepped inside the house.

Mrs. Roberts sat on a couch in the living room, a Kleenex in her hand. She had been crying. A woman Sam didn't recognize appeared to be consoling her.

"On what grounds are you here?" he asked. "My task force was put together years ago. We're handling this case."

"Not anymore," Hanover said in a firm, matter-of-fact tone.

"On what grounds?" He didn't want to get angry or have a confrontation with a fellow officer of the law, but he was so close to finishing this that he wouldn't let it go.

"An officer has been killed, and another officer assaulted. A member of the Ward family has been shot. Do you know how many agents are involved with the Ward family? An eighteen-year-old is out there." She stopped talking and turned away. Sam followed Agent Hanover's eyes. She was looking at Mrs. Roberts. "We will continue this conversation on the back deck," she said and walked away from Sam and Dolan.

Sam gritted his teeth and followed her. This was the first time he had ever been removed from a case. It felt disrespectful and pissed him off.

He stepped out onto the back deck behind Hanover. The wind had picked up. It tossed Agent Hanover's long blond hair into her face. She had to brush it aside to look at him.

"As I was saying," she continued. "We've got an eighteen-year-old girl out there with this maniac, and you still think this is just a kidnapping."

"I am quite aware of what's happening. I've been at this long enough to know what I'm doing. Within a couple of days, this will all be wrapped up. We don't need you interfering now."

"It's wrapped up now," Hanover said. "Are you aware of what the other officers are saying about you and your little psychic friend here?"

Sam looked over at Dolan, who leaned against the wooden deck railing. The strong eastern wind had its way with his short hair, too.

"I asked him to be here because he's helped us tremendously in the past. Without Dolan, some girls may not have made it home."

"It doesn't matter anymore," Hanover said. "You're both off this case. I'll need everything you have so far. Relinquish all your files to my partner Special Agent Fergus Mant, and don't even *think* about any Lone Ranger stuff, or you'll be dealing with obstruction charges. All the paperwork you need from us is at the front for you to sign when you leave."

Sam stormed off the deck. He heard Dolan close behind as he walked through the kitchen and down the hall to the front door.

Mike, his technician, came into view. Since the FBI no longer needed him at the Roberts house, Sam told Mike to ride with him and Dolan. Mike said he would meet them out front.

Sam paused in the living room and nodded at Mrs. Roberts. When he had started this case, he had promised to do whatever he could to bring Sarah home safely.

He was not about to give up.

He would keep his promise.

Chapter 48

AMELIA SAT ALONE ON the edge of her bed in a room at a Holiday Inn. Caleb had gone to lunch alone, and Tracy had gone to her room next door. The FBI psychologist had insisted they stay at the hotel in adjoining rooms. Apparently, the FBI had decided it would be better for the parents to be in a hotel rather than in their own home while the authorities worked the case.

Amelia knew this was only to help control Caleb. After his little performance last night, that new female FBI Agent Hanover wasn't going to have him hanging around the house, getting in the way.

Our house, she thought.

She got up and moved to the window. The wind had died down, the trees only bending slightly. In the distance, she could see a highway, trucks, and cars racing by. She wondered where Sarah was right now. Then she stopped herself. Thinking about Sarah only led to negative dark thoughts.

She moved away from the window and returned to the bed, where she flopped down. Sarah had saved Mary Bennett from a kidnapping. What was that all about, and why couldn't she save herself?

Mary was asked to lie for Sarah the night she was taken. What had her daughter been up to? Amelia used both hands to run through her hair in frustration as she realized she was thinking about Sarah again.

But how can't I?

A part of her felt that she knew nothing about her daughter, yet she had always thought she did.

After Sarah's diagnosis of depression and subsequent prescription of Zoloft, Amelia felt a deeper bond with Sarah. Evidently, her daughter had not shared the same connection.

Amelia hoped this would be all over soon. Life had to get back to some sort of reasonable control. How does a parent deal with losing both of her children to kidnappers?

Wasn't one enough? she thought, looking up at the roof of the hotel room.

The phone in the room rang.

She looked at it. Why would Caleb call her? He was just down the hall in the restaurant.

It rang again.

No one knew she was here but Caleb and the FBI. Tracy was in the next room.

The incessant ring came a third time. Amelia picked it up.

"Hello?"

At first, she heard nothing, then a distant sound. It was like the wind at the end of a tunnel.

A young female voice whispered, *"I'm okay now."*

The hairs on Amelia's neck rose, and she shivered as goosebumps roamed her arms. "Who is this?" she asked.

"Vivian."

She nearly slammed the phone down. What a cruel trick. Amelia wiped a tear away. She could hear someone knocking on the hotel room door.

"Who is this?" she shouted. Her eyes were wide but unseeing. Her heart beat a pulse through her entire body, and her breath came in gasps.

"Hi, Mommy," the soft female voice whispered. *"I'm okay. I'm with Sarah."*

"With Sarah? Does that mean … Sarah's dead?"

She almost went hysterical as she wondered why she was playing along with this. She switched the phone to her left hand and pressed it hard against her ear.

"She's alive."

The voice faded. The knocking on the hotel room door was a hammering now.

"A note will be left for you in a van."

The line went dead.

"Vivian! Vivian! Oh, my baby." Amelia collapsed on the floor, her body shaking with uncontrollable sobbing.

The hotel room door flew open. Caleb rushed in.

"What happened?" he asked. "Why were you screaming?"

He knelt and placed his arms around her. They held each other. Amelia could feel Tracy in the room. She wasn't going to talk to Caleb with the psychologist hanging around.

She felt Caleb move his hand, subtly asking Tracy to leave them alone.

Amelia heard the soft hush of the door shutting.

She looked up at her husband and told him everything. Whether he believed it or not, Amelia knew she had talked to her daughter. It was the maternal instinct God had given her.

If the line between sanity and insanity had been crossed, then she knew exactly what side of the line she was on.

And now she was determined to get out of this hotel room and find a van with a note in it.

Chapter 49

THE CRAMPS DOUBLED HER over. She had known hunger in the past, but not like this. Out of habit, she yanked hair away from inside the bandanna line. She could handle this. Try to ignore the pain. Think of better times.

She thought of what she had written down during the last blackout. It made her pull even more. Everything always felt better with the pulling.

Who cared anyway?

It didn't matter what she looked like. She had gone way too far in the years past with her pulling. Only stray patches remained on her head.

Getting those prophetic messages and then acting on them, she actually thought she was doing something good. She cared, but no one else did.

Look at the mess she was in now. She couldn't even remember how long she'd been with this kidnapping sadist.

Two days? Four days? Or could it be longer?

She leaned back and stretched out across the wooden bench. She placed her hands together on her stomach and shut her eyes. She imagined this was how she would look in her coffin. She didn't want to be the one to let go and give up, but what else was there? She would have to take it if she got a chance to run.

"You asleep back there, or are you having a blackout?"

She didn't answer him. With her eyes closed, he'd never know the difference. The currency of hope was almost paid out. This game of ruining lives he played was coming to an end. She could not get over that she had seen people killed. The cop on the highway, who probably had a family, didn't deserve to die. She could only get through this because of the automatic writing. Witnessing violence, injuries, and near-death situations for the last six months had changed her. Her current situation had changed her, too, but in a different way. It was like she was jaded now. She once heard that the only thing that separated humans from animals was their capacity to have hope. She no longer felt sure that she possessed hope. No hope meant she had nothing to lose.

"I've got to get gas. I'll pick up some take-out for us, too."

She felt the speed decrease, then came the gentle turn onto a gravel surface. When they stopped, the engine turned off. She kept her eyes closed and didn't move. She listened as he got out of his seat and made his way back toward her.

There was a moment of silence. She wanted to open her eyes to see what he was doing but realized the importance of remaining in her exact position. The interior of the van became silent.

A knock on the window made her jump. Her heart rate spiked along with her breathing. She tried hard to remain still.

Did he notice me jolt?

She could not risk opening her eyes.

She heard him shuffling to the front of the van. An attendant wanted to know if he could fill the van. The door opened, and she felt the vehicle move and adjust under Gert's weight as he exited the van.

This was her best chance. She was untied and unwatched. She could not be with Gert any longer. She couldn't handle more people dying.

This ends now.

She opened her eyes and got up. A Volkswagen van was parked ahead getting gas by a young brown-haired guy. He wore what looked like a gas station uniform with his name sewn into the left breast pocket.

She grabbed the pad of paper Gert had given her and removed the note she had written for her mother during the last blackout. A slot between the bench and the side of the van was a perfect fit. She left a small corner sticking out. It was just enough for someone to see if they were in the back but not enough for the driver to notice.

She folded the rest of the pad and slipped it into her pocket.

In a crouched position, she made her way toward the front. She kept her eyes glued to the windshield, looking for any sign of Gert. It wasn't until she reached the passenger seat that she saw him. He was inside the restaurant at the counter.

She opened the driver's side door and jumped down, her legs wobbly but strong enough to sustain her. She closed the door and crouched low.

The attendant smiled and nodded as he lifted the nozzle out of the Volkswagen. She waved for him to come over.

"What can I do for you?" he asked.

He stared at her eyebrows. The makeup she used to paint them on would have faded by now. Her clothes were in disarray, and she probably looked dirty and gaunt.

Her eyes watered as she fought back the tears.

What a horrible time to start crying, she thought.

"I've been … kidnapped. You've got to help me. My name is Sarah Roberts. That man who asked you to fill up the van is a murderer. He killed a cop on the highway …" Then she thought of something that would explain how she looked. "Look what he's already done to me. He's torturing me by slowly pulling all my hair out." She tugged on his sleeve. "Please help. Call the police."

"Okay, slow down. I do recall they were looking for a guy who kidnapped a girl. I saw the cover of today's newspaper in the box over there." He pointed.

"He'll be coming back any minute. I have to be gone, or he'll kill me."

"Hold on. I'll just pick up a phone and tell him I'm calling the police. He won't do anything crazy in public. You hide behind a car at the back of the building or something. Just stay hidden."

"No, no, you can't. Don't you understand? He has nothing to lose." She looked at the inside counter where she had seen him moments before, but he was gone. "He doesn't care. He won't hesitate to kill you, too."

This wasn't working. She told him to call the police discreetly as soon as he could. Then she hobbled away. She stumbled on her weak limbs but managed to maintain her balance.

Exposed, out in the open, she gave it her all. The tree line would provide cover.

Twenty more steps.

She looked to her right. Cars raced by on the highway. People in their own world, completely unaware an eighteen-year-old was running for her life.

Panic set in. She could feel it. Her breath hitched in her throat. She felt eyes on her. She anticipated a bullet in the back at any moment.

She didn't waste time looking over her shoulder. If he saw her making a break for it, then he would give chase or shoot her.

She would either make the cover of the trees or be shot, which amounted to this ordeal ending. Something about death seemed desirable, like food. She was so hungry she could taste the smell coming from the gas station's restaurant, her mouth chewing imaginary food.

Leaves and branches brushed her arms as she dropped down a small three-foot embankment. The cover of trees swallowed her. She stopped about ten feet in to fall to her knees and catch a breath.

She listened to determine if someone was pursuing her. She peeked through the branches by pulling one down. The gas attendant was out of sight. Gert was nowhere to be seen.

She made it. She had escaped. A wave of relief washed over her. Could this really be done?

She decided to wait in the trees for a few hours. She could wait until the cover of darkness or come out when the police arrived. She could lie down and sleep on a bed of leaves.

Then the gas attendant appeared at the side of the van pulling the nozzle out and replacing the gas cap. He looked her way once before walking around to the front and heading for the restaurant.

Gert came into view.

She ducked her head down. Being blind was worse. She pulled on a branch and raised herself enough to look across the parking lot.

She could see Gert and the attendant talking. Gert was shaking his head.

Sarah started deeper into the thicket. This was over for her. She was determined to put as much geography between her and Gert as she could.

***

"You're all filled up, sir. It came to fifty-eight dollars."

Gert studied the guy. He looked to be around seventeen. Something was wrong with the guy, though. The kid's eyes shifted past Gert's shoulder, then trained back on Gert, then over to the pumps and onto a car going by on the highway. He rubbed his hands together and looked down at them like the grease stains were suddenly very interesting. Maybe the kid noticed the bulge of the gun under Gert's shirt and recognized it for what it was.

Gert guessed they were about six feet from the van.

Could this kid have talked to Sarah?

He kept his eyes on the nervous kid while he stepped back to look in the van's windows. He set the bag of food on the concrete and cupped his hands around his eyes to see to the back.

Sarah was gone.

Shit.

He spun around, accidentally kicked the paper bag of greasy burgers, and pulled his gun.

The gas jockey was already running.

He almost made it to the safety of the restaurant.

***

A loud crack in the air told Sarah that a gun had been fired.

A high-pitched scream followed.

She stopped running. Her breath came out in waves.

Someone was probably calling the police by now. Could she trust the police? Gert's boss worked with them. Her priority had to be her mother. Somehow, she had to contact her mother.

She decided she had to see for herself what was going on.

She saved people. *That's* who Sarah was.

Without that, she was better off dead.

***

Gert walked toward the attendant, his gun extended in front of him. People were running for cover. A car squealed out of the parking lot behind him.

When he got close to the gas jockey, he saw a flesh wound on the kid's right calf muscle. He noticed the kid's name tag said Steve.

"Where is she?"

Steve lay there with both hands on his wounded leg. Small rivers of blood seeped through his fingers. He responded with only grunts and groans.

Gert got down on his knees and pulled the kid's face close to his. He pressed the gun to the underside of Steve's jaw.

"I won't ask again," Gert said. "Where is she?"

Steve's eyes rolled in his head as he fainted. Gert let go of him and stood.

He could see no sign of Sarah anywhere.

He had lost her again.

Someone yelled inside the restaurant.

Gert gritted his teeth. He raised the gun in the air and fired randomly.

"Sarah! Come out, come out, wherever you are. How many people have to die for you?"

***

Sarah ducked at the sound of gunfire. She was close enough to hear Gert hollering.

She peeked through branches and saw Gert standing halfway between the van and the restaurant. The gas jockey was on the ground.

He wasn't moving. She saw blood pooling below his waist.

This can't be happening. How crazy is this guy?

She let go of the branch and looked down at her hairless forearms. She was in over her head. She could never let Gert have her again. She had no idea what to do next.

Is this what absolute hopelessness feels like?

She leaned sideways against a small tree. Her body was reacting to the stress in ways she wasn't familiar with—ragged breath, weakness in her stomach and legs, and a heart that seemed out of rhythm.

She had nothing in her stomach to throw up, but it felt like something was coming.

She sat down on the dead-leaf-covered ground, dropped her face into her hands, and lost her last bit of control.

She broke down with a deep feeling of despair.

***

Gert raised his gun and fired through one of the restaurant's front windows.

He was careful to aim for the top of the main window as he didn't want to be known as a mass murderer. If his brother were alive, he would be proud of his restraint.

"That's another one dead," he yelled.

He fired into the roof of the restaurant. "And yet another one bites the dust. How many people have to be shot for your freedom, Sarah?"

Someone was running behind him, footsteps pounding the pavement.

He pivoted on the spot and saw Sarah making a break for the highway. As she hit the shoulder of the road, she lost her balance and tumbled forward, rolling directly in front of a large oil tanker.

The truck swerved.

Its horn blared as the driver got his vehicle back under control. Brake lights came on. The oil tanker was stopping, pulling over.

Gert dropped the gun to his side.

Looks like Sarah wants to get run over.

He started walking to the highway. *This ought to be amusing*, he thought with a wry smile.

***

Sarah's right shoulder screamed. When she lost her footing and fell, the gravel dug in, lacerating her skin.

She scanned the road in both directions. Only two cars were coming, one from either direction. The oil tanker guy was climbing down from his cab.

She looked back at the gas station and saw Gert walking toward her.

Never again, she thought as she got up and put one foot in front of the other.

She touched the tender area of her shoulder. Her hand came away with blood on it.

Why isn't he shooting me?

Maybe he thought she tried suicide by throwing herself in front of the truck.

A large black car approached. The vehicle wasn't slowing down. She stepped into the middle of the highway. She closed her eyes tight. Her shoulder felt aflame now. It felt like the pebbles embedded in her flesh were digging deeper. She focused on the pain and waited.

She could hear the car slowing fast, its tires gripping the hot pavement.

"Are you okay?"

It wasn't Gert's voice. She opened her eyes.

"Help me. Please take me to a hospital. They've tortured me, pulled my hair out."

"What? Hold on."

A large black man opened the door and stepped out.

"What's your name?"

***

Gert couldn't believe it.

Some guy had stopped his car and was talking to her. The oil tanker driver was almost upon her, too.

He couldn't allow a stranger to take Sarah away. He broke into a run.

"Hey!" Gert shouted.

The tall black guy turned and looked at him. Sarah threw herself into the back seat of the car. From fifty yards away, he could hear Sarah yelling for the guy to get in and drive.

She was completely inside someone else's car now.

He raised his gun and fired. The bullet missed the guy. A hole formed beside him in the open driver's door window. That was enough to get the guy moving.

Gert fired again as the driver slammed his door shut. Gert was close enough now to see the guy's hand pull the transmission down. The car lurched forward, away from Gert and the gas station.

It took Gert precious seconds to get back to the van.

When he started it and turned toward the highway, the black car had disappeared.

Chapter 50

SARAH SCRAMBLED AROUND IN the back seat and got into a crouched position, careful to avoid her wounded shoulder touching anything. She took a quick look out the rear window. No sign of Gert's van in pursuit.

"What was with that guy?" the driver asked. "Why would he shoot at us?"

Sarah could detect a slight southern accent. She looked at the driver's eyes in the rearview mirror.

"You okay, girl?" he asked.

"He kidnapped me a few days ago. Please, just get me to a phone, then leave."

"Is that the guy they're searching for? A manhunt, the newspapers called it."

Sarah nodded. The driver mumbled something to himself.

"Don't worry," Sarah said. "You won't be mixed up in this if you just get me to a phone and take off."

"But he killed a cop and apparently two members of a crime family out of New York. This morning's paper said *armed and dangerous*."

The driver kept darting his eyes between the road ahead and his mirrors.

There was still no sign of the van behind them. She looked at the back of the driver's head. "He will be coming after me. He won't let me get away that easy. You need to go faster."

She examined her shoulder. The scattered dirt and small pebbles were easily brushed off. The bleeding was minimal, but it hurt like a bitch.

Asphalt raced by under the car, open empty fields by the windows. This would never be over until she was home with her parents, and Gert was either locked up or dead.

Every mile counted. They crested a rise and saw a small town coming up. The driver swung into a convenience store and gas station on the right.

"You're safe now," he said. "This is where you get out. They'll let you use their phone inside."

She mumbled her thanks as she exited the car. He stayed in the parking lot and watched her until she entered the store.

An Asian man stood behind the counter.

"I need to use a phone," Sarah said. "It's an emergency."

She saw the clerk's smile fade and then disappear. He stared at her, taking in her appearance. She looked like she had just walked away from an explosion in the sewer system.

"Please, your phone?"

The door swung open behind her. It was the driver who brought her here. "The black van is coming."

The driver turned around and flipped the interior thumb lock on the door, locking it from the inside. The Asian man behind the counter protested.

"Get away from the windows," the driver told her. "You too," he said to the clerk.

A vehicle pulled into the parking lot out front. She could hear it sliding to a stop on the gravel as she ran for the back of the store. On the way, she grabbed a handful of Twinkies and a Red Bull from a corner display.

The first door she came to open into a stock room. They stepped through it. The driver stood by the door, leaving it ajar as Sarah walked to the back loading area and quietly unlocked it without opening it. By this time, she had stuffed one full Twinkie in her mouth. It tasted like a gourmet meal.

A gun went off, followed by shattered glass. The driver shut the door he was peeking through and ran for Sarah.

"Open it, open it," he said. "We gotta get outta here."

She pushed down on the bar and yanked open the back door. A loud buzzer sounded. They had set off an alarm. Gert would know she was leaving through the back door and be on them in no time.

Back in the sunlight, there was no time for indecision. A dumpster sat twenty feet away on her left.

The driver grabbed her arm. He was panicking. She saw his eyes darting back and forth. Which way to go? Already precious seconds were lost.

The driver freaked and started running. He headed for the open field behind the store.

"No, he'll see you," she called after him.

Sarah bolted for the dumpster. She grabbed the open lid and swung it shut with a loud bang. Then she turned and ran around the building.

She hoped Gert would waste precious time talking to an empty dumpster thinking she or the driver was in it.

Scrunching herself against the building wall, she brushed sweat from her eyes as she looked around the corner. Only the black van and the car that brought her here sat out front.

She couldn't believe her luck. The car that brought her here was idling. She jammed another Twinkie into her mouth and popped open the Red Bull.

Gert was in the back of the building looking for her, and in the distance, she could hear a police siren. The store owner must have hit a buzzer or called them. Or maybe they were called when the back door alarm triggered.

She distrusted the cops.

Gert's boss worked with the cops.

She pushed away from her hiding place and ran for the idling car, her heart beating in harmony with the pounding of her feet. Her second wind had kicked in. She hadn't felt this alive in days. The Twinkies were at work. The tables had turned. She was back in charge, being proactive, saving someone.

Saving myself.

The vehicle was an automatic. In seconds Sarah was on the highway, the wind caressing her face through the open driver's side window as she finished the Red Bull. She tried to keep the car steady, narrowly missing a station wagon going the other way.

She had limited experience behind the wheel, yet she carefully maneuvered her way into the little town.

No bullets pursued her.

Chapter 51

Gert had had enough. A siren wailed in the distance. He held his gun up and opened the top of the garbage dumpster.

It was empty.

"Fuck," he said to himself.

He did a complete turn, looking at all points of the compass. Nothing but open fields. Maybe he missed them in the store after all. He rushed back in. A quick but thorough search told him the store was completely empty. Even the clerk had bolted.

The siren was closer.

"Fuck, shit."

He had lost Sarah for good this time. The cops were coming. He wasn't going to die in a stupid convenience store on the side of the highway.

He ran for the van. When he got in and started it up, he noticed the car was gone. The guy who picked Sarah up in front of the gas station must have left. She was probably with him. They would be at the police station in no time, giving a description of him and the vehicle he was in.

It was over.

Sarah had finally gotten away.

That fucking bitch.

Gert pounded the steering wheel as he did a U-turn and raced up the highway the way he had come. He would pass the gas station again. No one ever expected the bad guy to return to the crime scene. It was better than driving into the small town behind him and possibly getting trapped by some local cops.

After less than a minute, before he lost the convenience store from sight in his rearview mirror, he saw a lone cruiser pull into its parking lot, lights blazing.

Minutes later, he drove past the gas station. Police cars were already there, with cops standing around talking to people from the restaurant.

Someone was pointing down the road the way Gert had just come from.

No one looked at him as he passed.

He had a head start with no idea where he was going. There was no plan. His brother would know what to do, but his brother was dead.

Change vehicles. That was something he could do.

There was nothing left but to run.

Unless he could get another hostage.

Chapter 52

Sam Johnson glanced at Dolan as they listened to the police radio. There had been a shooting at a gas station off the highway. The dispatcher was calling for all units in the area to attend.

Dolan nodded to confirm it was the guy they were looking for—the guy who had Sarah.

The authorities would cordon off the area. The perp was as good as caught. Sam hoped Sarah would walk away unharmed.

He threw his coffee out the window, started the unmarked cruiser, and headed toward the gas station.

They had been discussing their next move. Sam didn't want to go against the FBI, but with how close they were to catching this guy and what they already knew of the case, it was too late to give up and let the FBI take over. He had been the head of the task force for long enough to handle this case until completion.

Dolan was advising him to move on. Pack up and do something else. Tangling with this case further could only spell trouble. But Sam needed closure. He needed to find out how this perp always seemed to get away. Why was he one step ahead? As Mary Bennett said, Sarah had stopped a kidnapping in the past, so why didn't she stop her own?

Then there was Dolan to consider.

"Dolan, tell me something."

"What?"

"Why do you think this case is different from any other kidnappings?"

Sam could feel Dolan watching him as he drove.

"How do you mean different?"

"This is the first time I've seen you come up short. I mean, you didn't get us to the cabin on time. Now you know the perp is involved in the gas station mess, but you didn't mention it—not until it had happened."

He snuck a glance at Dolan, who was rubbing his forehead as he looked out at the passing countryside.

"I don't know. I can only speculate."

"Speculate then," Sam said.

"It might be different because I'm involved."

"What do you mean? You're always involved."

"I mean, I'm physically in this cruiser, and I went to the cabin. A psychic can't read their own future. If I did, I'd be able to pick the next winning lottery numbers."

Dolan's cell rang. Sam watched for the exit to take him east on Interstate 29 while Dolan mumbled into his phone where he was going.

When he flipped it shut, Sam looked over. "Who was that? You told the caller about the gas station."

"That was Alex, my assistant at the psychic fair. It's closed for two weeks until we get to the next city and set up. He had nothing to do, so I told him we would be at the gas station crime scene so he could come and get me. It sounds like this is coming to an end soon, anyway. Alex has a certain talent himself. Since he's not directly involved or helping on this case, he may have some information for you."

Sam could detect a little sarcasm in Dolan's voice. He couldn't be sure if it was intentional or not.

"If you're saying your physical presence might stop you from being psychic, maybe you'll have more information yourself since you won't be directly involved anymore."

"Just drive, Sam. We've worked together too long to fight."

Chapter 53

GERT HAD TO CHANGE vehicles as soon as possible or dump this one and hole up somewhere safe.

His cell battery had died hours ago, leaving him no way to call the boss for help. Hands-on cash was running low. Using a debit or credit card right now would alert anyone looking for him.

He reminded himself that, at this precise moment, not all the cops would know Sarah wasn't with him anymore. For at least the next hour, they might not shoot on sight.

A long train was crossing the grassy fields ahead. A flashing red light alerted Gert to stop.

He saw his luck in the form of a BMW SUV stopped at the railway crossing. It was the only vehicle. The train moved slowly over the two-lane highway. If he were quick, there would be enough time to do what he needed.

He pulled up behind the SUV. Then, with a quick foot, he shot the van forward and then slammed the brake hard. It was a perfect hit, just enough to smack the BMW SUV but not enough to leave a broken bumper or worse.

The driver got out at the same time Gert did, and he saw it was a lone female with long brown hair, mid-forties, unsteady on high heels.

"What happened?" she asked. "You couldn't see I was stopped?" The woman bent to inspect the damage.

"I'm sorry. My foot slipped. I went to tap the brake but hit the accelerator instead."

"Well, it doesn't look as bad as I thought."

Gert pulled out his weapon.

"Step away from the vehicle."

The woman turned and saw the gun. She tried to step back, but Gert was already grabbing her lapel. He dragged her close to him, the gun pressed into her abdomen. The expression on her face was priceless.

"We're going to play a little game," he said. "I'll take your BMW, and you drive my van. I'll give you a two-minute head start, and then the chase begins."

"What ... what chase?"

Her voice cracked. Gert would never get sick of how people reacted to him. He loved her quivering weakness.

"I chase you. If I catch you, you die. It's that simple. Don't stop for anyone. Don't slow down. Whatever you do, don't let me catch you."

"Why are you doing this?"

"Because I can. Now get in the van. I left it running."

Gert pushed her away from him. She stumbled to the door of the van.

"Go that way," Gert said, pointing where he had just come from. "Don't let me catch you. I'll give you a two-minute head start, so drive fast."

He kept the gun pointed at her as she got in the van. He heard the transmission shift into gear. When she looked at him through the windshield, he made a display of looking at his wrist to remind her of the time limit.

She turned the van around and started away from him. He knew she would be watching in the mirrors, so he raised the gun and fired a warning shot into the van's back window on the passenger side.

The vehicle skidded back and forth a little and then took off. She must have dropped the pedal all the way down.

Gert hopped into the BMW and did a three-point turn to aim after her. When the van was lost to sight, and the train had cleared the tracks, he turned the BMW back around and floored it in the opposite direction.

Chapter 54

It took Sarah a moment to realize she was alone in the front seat of a car and not with her kidnapper.

She must've blacked out.

She had pulled into a gas station parking area after a cop car passed her with its lights and siren on. She had wanted to stick around to see Gert get arrested. What she saw was the black van drive away unnoticed by the police.

She looked at her right arm while rubbing it. The familiar numbness was there. Did she write something? She looked around for anything she would have been able to write on. A newspaper sat folded beside her. Sketched in her handwriting in the margin was a note:

... drive after van ... twenty minutes left to stop another kill ... only you can stop Gert's boss ...

Sarah started the car and got back on the highway.

She headed out of town as fast as she could without speeding. She looked down and saw a small stash of coins in the ashtray. A pack of gum was in the glove box, which she unwrapped and tossed in her mouth. The taste was incredible. She chewed with fervor, savoring every swallow of gum juice.

The note said twenty minutes were left to stop another kill.

She could just turn the car around and call home. She had won her freedom. She examined why she chose to head back into the fray and realized she had no other choice.

She is the one who gets the messages. She would never forget finding the first few notes after coming out of what she knew now was *an episode* almost seven months ago. Her arm had been numb, which is something she had come to realize was a warning sign.

She had bumped her head when her first blackout had come upon her. A note that someone had written, which she later figured out was her own doing, sat on the floor beside her. It said something about a teenager a block away needing help and to call the police on the girl's father.

She couldn't remember the exact words because she crumpled it up after reading the note and threw it away.

The next day she heard that a fifteen-year-old girl got beat up by her father on their front lawn. Sarah asked around the neighborhood to learn more about what had happened. Apparently, the teenage girl was dating a guy much older, and since she refused to stop seeing him, her dad had thought he would teach her a lesson. The father was known to police, she learned later, and a professional alcoholic.

They lived a block away. Sarah could have intervened with a phone call.

After that incident, Sarah stopped throwing the notes away. She had started carrying paper everywhere and eventually upgraded to a notebook.

After her intervention prevented Mary Bennett's kidnapping, she had sworn to act on any message as best as possible. She would at least try if it were in her power to help someone. She toyed with the idea that she had been chosen for this.

The thought of being chosen made her feel special, even powerful. It also gave her purpose like she had never felt before. It was like she had an arrangement with God. He would protect her. He would take care of her. This was His deal.

If she was the only one who could stop Gert, then she had to try. The messages had never been wrong before.

At the moment, she was wide awake, still breathing and feeling strong after the burst of sugar and caffeine.

The gas station where she escaped from the van passed on her right, and then it was in her mirrors. She was doing over sixty-five miles an hour. Multiple police vehicles, ambulances, and dark-colored sedans littered the parking lot. She checked her mirrors, but no one was coming after her. No one at the scene would be distracted by the prospect of handing out a speeding ticket.

The black van Gert had held her captive popped up about a mile ahead, coming toward her. Sarah let off the accelerator a little. From this distance, she could see the van was moving fast.

She eased up more. Why would Gert be driving like that? Why would he return to the gas station, where countless people could identify him and the vehicle he was driving?

Something told her the driver of the van was no longer Gert.

The black van was half a mile away and closing fast. Sarah slowed down and steered the car as far to the right as she could go without driving on the shoulder.

She saw long hair through the windshield when the van got close enough. The driver was female.

Maybe it's just another black van, she thought.

She saw a small hole surrounded by concentric lines in the windshield as the driver raced by her.

A bullet hole.

Sarah could see the woman was doing at least eighty miles an hour. That might catch someone's attention at the gas station.

But then, what vehicle was Gert in now? How would she ever know with ten minutes left in her recent prophecy?

She hit the gas and pushed the car as fast as she dared without losing control.

Chapter 55

Sam signaled and pulled over onto the shoulder. When the car had come to a complete stop, he opened his door and got out.

"What're you doing?" Dolan asked.

"Get out."

Dolan hesitated, then opened his door and stepped from the car. They looked at each other over the roof.

The last thing Sam wanted for his career was to show up at the gas station crime scene with the *psychic* in tow. The way FBI Agent Hanover talked about Dolan, it could harm Sam's ability to be taken seriously, even though Dolan had proven to be a big help in the past.

"Dolan, you're not leveling with me. There's something you're not telling me. I don't have to be psychic to know you're acting differently in this case. We've talked about it, but I must be upfront. I'm not showing my face at that gas station crime scene with you. Call Alex and get him to pick you up here."

Dolan rested his forearms on the open car door and lowered his head. He adjusted his sunglasses and looked back up. "I don't know what it is either. Maybe it's because I don't want to do this anymore. Perhaps I'm psychically not as available as I used to be." A soft breeze moved his hair. "Sam, I can't handle the naggers. Those people who read about my successes with the police department and then swamp the psychic fair." He raised his hands, palms out. "I know, I know, isn't that what I want—the more visitors at the fair, the better. The problem is, everyone wants me to do their reading."

Sam waited for a small sports car to pass behind him. His jacket rustled in its wake. "So let me get this straight, you agree to help find Sarah, but you don't want to do it. Then, while you're supposedly helping to find a kidnapped teenager, you're allowing your personal wants and needs to get in the way."

"Saying it that way makes me sound like a letch. Sam, you're interpreting it wrong. It's true. I don't want to do this anymore. I didn't want to help when Sarah's father came and asked me. But after thinking it over and talking to Esmerelda, I decided I would help you guys again."

Sam looked over his shoulder as a rig passed by. Dolan walked around the back of the car and stepped closer to Sam. "But you know as well as I do when I agree to take on something, I give it my best. My inability to help this time has nothing to do with personal feelings." He reached into his back pocket and pulled out a piece of paper. "Here, look at this."

Sam took the note and flipped it over. It was from Sarah. "What's this? How long have you had it?"

"Since I first got to the Roberts's house. Sarah has a gift, too. She knew I'd search her room. In my opinion, she may be the one blocking me, but not intentionally. This is her gig. That's how she saved Mary Bennett and others over the last six months."

Sam stepped away from him. "Are you trying to tell me that an eighteen-year-old girl thinks she's talking to someone on the Other Side and then going out and saving strangers from trouble with these messages, all the while putting herself in very risky situations where she could be killed? This is the version you believe?"

"I don't know what Sarah is yet. Not until I talk to her."

Sam looked at the note in his hand. People were dead. A cop was killed, and another was assaulted. Sam refused to believe that Sarah somehow would have prior knowledge of some events and not others. If she was, in fact, helping to stop kidnappings, then how did *she* get taken? He believed it went deeper than what her notebook revealed.

"Gun!"

He jumped and ducked his head out of reflex as Dolan screamed the word *gun*. Sam landed on the cruiser's hood without thinking, trying for the safety of the other side. He saw Dolan making his way around the trunk.

Sam caught a glimpse of the road as he slid off the other side of the hood. An SUV was headed directly for them, its driver's side window down. A gun protruded out, aimed in their direction.

Just as the BMW was drawing level, a four-door Impala bumped the BMW from behind.

The gun went off, but the Impala's impact spoiled the shooter's aim. The bullet meant for Sam lodged in the windshield of his cruiser, an inch above the wiper.

The driver of the BMW took another wild shot but hit nothing as he passed them. Sam saw the gun hand withdraw into the driver's window. The BMW raced away from them while the Impala slowed down and stopped on the opposite shoulder.

The moment's intensity had his heart beating to a soldier's stomp. Sam drew his sidearm and stepped toward the Impala.

"Get out of the vehicle, hands where I can see them," he shouted.

The door opened. A thin, frail-looking girl turned in the driver's seat and tried to stand. Sam approached with caution, his internal radar pinging.

"I'm Sarah Roberts. The man who tried to shoot you was my kidnapper. I would've called after I got away from him, but I received a message that you would be killed. I guess I got here just in time." She smiled.

Chapter 56

Special Agent Jill Hanover pulled into one of America's last Texaco gas stations. She parked her Crown Victoria under the old, weathered sign that had seen more summer sun than a beach.

Fergus Mant jumped out of the passenger seat and asked who was in charge. Hanover overheard him promptly tell someone that the FBI had arrived and was taking over the crime scene.

A moment later, Hanover's forensics van pulled in and parked by the restaurant doors.

She hustled over and told Angus Tran to make sure nothing got missed.

"I want every shell casing, every fingerprint. I especially want everyone here to give a full statement before they leave. Nothing gets missed."

"Understood," Tran nodded and skirted away.

Two ambulances and five marked police cars littered the Texaco parking lot. The immediate area was filled with people contaminating evidence.

She headed for the restaurant entrance, where she saw Fergus arguing with a uniformed officer.

"Fergus, make sure nothing gets missed. Find out who showed up on the scene first and get everything you can from them. If the guy bought gas, I want to know about it. Get prints from the counter where he would have paid. If they have any kind of cameras in this joint, I want the footage."

Tran interrupted her. "Agent Hanover, we just got a call that a black van was pulled over a couple of miles from here. It matches the description of the one reported stolen yesterday and the one people here said they saw. State troopers spotted it easily because of the van's speed."

"Did they nab the guy? Is Sarah with him?"

"The perp had switched vehicles. The van's driver is a woman who said he was chasing her in *her* BMW. It was some kind of game he set up."

"Did this woman get a good look at the perp?"

"Up close," Tran was nodding. "But here's the good part. The carjacker was alone. He didn't have a girl with him. That jives with what a few of the witnesses are saying here. The girl ran onto the highway and was picked up by a guy driving an Impala. Sarah may have gotten away."

Hanover turned to Fergus. "I need you to radio our Hostage Rescue Team and the negotiator. Bring them up to speed on what's happening. We'll have to keep them mobile until we get a lock on the victim and the perp."

She looked back at Tran. "Is the helicopter up yet?"

"Yes," Tran said and referred to his watch. "It'll be in the area in fifteen minutes."

"Okay, put out a call to every law enforcement agency in the state to be on the lookout for this woman's BMW. Inform the helicopter pilot to maintain air support at fifteen hundred feet and wait for our call about the location of the perp."

Tran looked down at the paper he had been reading from. "There's one more thing. One of the officers who pulled the van over found a piece of paper by a bench in the back. It was addressed to Amelia Roberts. It appears to be from her daughter."

"What'd it say?"

"Usual endearment stuff," Tran said as he turned and went back to the gas pump area.

Hanover wanted to get in her car and look for this BMW herself, but the amount of work at the gas station kept her from it.

She turned when she saw Tran moving toward her again.

"You're not going to like what just came through the radio."

"Hit me with it."

"Sam Johnson is in pursuit of the perp as we speak."

"You don't mean the same Sam Johnson who ran the kidnapping task force, do you? The one I told was off this case? Tell me you don't mean him."

"The same one. But listen, it gets better. Dolan has Sarah Roberts. They're meeting with his assistant and then coming here." Tran looked at his watch. "They should be here in less than twenty minutes."

"Okay, now that's good news. Well, this is wrapping up quickly. We have to go. We leave in one minute. You come with me to navigate. I'll leave Fergus in charge here. Get someone to call Tracy at the Holiday Inn and tell her to get Sarah's parents out here. They're gonna want to meet up with their daughter. Find out where Sam is so we can help him stop this lunatic. Update the helicopter pilot, too. Let's move, let's move."

"On it," Tran said as he turned and ran.

Chapter 57

Gert pushed the power button on the car phone built into the dash of the BMW. Little lights illuminated as he dialed his boss. The phone was answered on the first ring.

"How do I get out of this?" Gert yelled into the phone. "Tell me what to do."

"Where're you?" his boss asked. "Why did you let this get so out of hand? Do you know how many law enforcement agencies are looking for you?"

"I would've never shot those guys behind the motel if you hadn't told me to go back and secure my hostage. It's your fault that I'm in this. It would've been one dead cop on the side of the highway and me long gone. But no, I had to take care of Sarah."

Gert gunned the BMW to pass a rig doing the speed limit.

"You don't have Sarah anymore. She gave you power, a position of bargaining. Now they've got her, and she knows about us. Sarah still has to be removed, and it looks like you will, too, without my help. Every cop for a thousand miles wants to put a bullet in you."

Gert pressed the phone hard against his ear. His suspicion was right. He could hear the engine sound of a car. The boss was driving. "Where're you? Is anyone in the car with you?"

"I'm alone, and I'm in your vicinity."

"What are you doing out here?"

"You've got a tail. A helicopter should be on your ass within a couple of minutes. I came to help, but I don't know how just yet. Tell me where you are so I can come and get you. The police are looking for the BMW you're in. They are not looking for my car. Your only way out of this is to get into my car."

Gert pulled the phone away from his ear. He smacked it on the dash three times. "You hear that? That's how it'll sound like when I'm smacking your head. You have no idea how frustrated I am right now."

"Okay, listen to me and listen carefully. I will be with Sarah shortly. The famed psychic has her, and he called in his location for a pick-up. Tell me where you are, and I'll bring them to you. We can finish this right."

Gert relayed the highway number he was on and the name of an exit ramp. He took the ramp and told his boss to look for a building with a BMW SUV parked out front. He would try to find something within a couple of miles from the ramp on the right side to hole up in.

"Take care of yourself, and don't get caught. I'll handle the girl and the psychic. See you soon."

Gert clicked off the BMW's built-in cell phone.

While talking to the boss, he noticed the distant sound of a helicopter approaching from behind him.

Chapter 58

DOLAN LOOKED UP AT the sound of a vehicle. Alex's silver Honda slowed and stopped a few feet from them. Over the last ten minutes, a dismal cloud cover had made its way above them. A soft drizzle started to fall, leaving a film of wetness on their skin. It felt like a cleansing, a cool break from the sun.

Dolan opened the back door for Sarah and helped her in. Then he jumped in the front and slammed the door.

"Thanks for coming to get us," Dolan said.

"No problem," Alex said. "I brought some food and a drink for Sarah."

He lifted a lunch bag over the seat and handed it to her, followed by two water bottles. "That should be good until we can get you to a hospital. How're you feeling? It must've been quite the ordeal."

"I'm okay," Sarah said. "Don't take me to a hospital just yet. Not until we catch up with the asshole that kidnapped me." Sarah tore open the lunch bag. "And what's that smell? Cologne of some kind?"

Dolan and Alex looked at each other. A big truck passed them, causing the little Honda to shake.

"We're not taking her to safety?" Alex asked.

Dolan had worked with Alex for years but hadn't seen this edge in him. Looking closer, Alex was actually shaking.

"No, not just yet. We need to be near the apprehension of the kidnapper. Sarah has information about the kidnapper's boss."

Alex jolted and then adjusted himself in his seat.

"You okay, Alex? Is this too much for you?"

"No, no, I'm fine. I've just never been this close to the action. You're the one who works with the police out in the field while I'm at the fair. So, understandably, I'm a little out of my element."

Dolan nodded in understanding, still harboring doubt. Something else was on his assistant's mind.

Alex put the vehicle in gear and merged back onto the two-lane highway. Dolan gave him directions to the Texaco station, where the police were converging.

Dolan needed to think about what Sarah had told him when they were waiting on the side of the highway. She had spoken about her powers and how the information came to her. She had told him details regarding the people she had saved so far. He remembered reading about her a couple of times in the newspaper because the police had linked her with two different incidents. The cop who responded to the car that flipped over the bridge and into the river was the same officer who showed up on the scene of a beating at a baseball diamond. He had claimed to recognize the girl because of her appearance and the bandanna on her head.

Dolan had asked Sarah how she knew the exact details of the beating incident at the baseball diamond. She said it was all written in the note. All she had to do was be on Meadowvale Street before 9:00 p.m. and stand by the baseball diamond with an aluminum bat. Step from the dug-out area on the home team side at 9:02 p.m. and swing the bat with all her strength in the midsection area. It was already dark, but when her watch turned to 9:02 p.m., she did just that.

The police were twenty paces behind the guy she knocked the wind out of. He would have gotten away had it not been for her. Sarah told Dolan that this venture into the night with a baseball bat had scared her more than any of the others. But she had committed with blind faith, knowing the message giver was not putting her in harm's way as long as she did exactly what the note said.

Dolan pondered all this while still trying to figure out why he had agreed to let her continue this dangerous search. Someone out there was the kidnapper's boss, and according to Sarah, she was the only one who could stop him.

Alex said they were coming up to the gas station soon. Dolan pulled out his cell phone and speed-dialed Sam. They talked briefly, and then he hung up.

"Looks like he followed the guy to an abandoned farmhouse …" Dolan trailed off when he saw the gun.

"I know where it is," Alex said. "I'd guess we're about five minutes from there."

"What're you doing?" Dolan asked.

"It's been a long time coming. I've envied you, looked up to you. But you've always put me down. Treated me like second class. I could've helped the police, too. I could've participated more, but no, you get all the fame, and then you whine about it. *Too many people want readings*, you say. You even have a name for them."

"Look, Alex, I don't think this is the right time to go through an employment issue."

"Employment issue? *Employment issue?* Is that what you think this is all about? Wow, then you really are a fucking head case."

Alex cleared his throat. Dolan kept his eyes on the gun. The Texaco passed by without Alex slowing the Honda. Dolan didn't want to play the role of a hero, and he hoped Sarah wouldn't either.

"For the past few years, I fed you information on the whereabouts of kidnap victims because I *knew* where they were. I thought you'd think I had great psychic powers, but you never did. You just told the authorities where the girls were and took the credit."

Dolan kept his hands where Alex could see them. "Are you saying you're the boss of this asshole that kidnapped Sarah?"

"You're getting it now. You win the prize in the box of pink popcorn." Alex looked sideways at him. "Just wait until everyone hears that your psychic fair has been involved with all the kidnappings so that you'll look psychic. With Sarah dead and the FBI about to kill Gert, I only need to remove you."

"Sarah dead? How do you intend to do that?"

Dolan realized the look he saw in Alex's eyes earlier wasn't fear. It was insanity.

"Pull out your cell phone. Do it slowly."

Dolan did as he was told while Alex tried to keep his eyes on the road and watch him simultaneously.

"Now toss it out the window."

Dolan complied. He wanted to snatch a look back at Sarah but couldn't risk it.

Alex checked his mirror and then applied the brake.

"What're you doing now?" Dolan asked.

"Letting you out."

"I'm not leaving Sarah alone with you."

Alex brought the Honda to a complete stop. "You don't have a choice. Get out."

Dolan folded his arms and looked straight out the windshield, portraying an image of defiance.

Sarah's scream accompanied the loud report of the gun. Dolan felt like he had been punched in the side by a sledgehammer. He looked down and saw a red dot on his left side. The dot was spreading fast. He looked up at Alex. Now his eyes held a cool resolve, the insanity behind them brewing.

"Head or gut. I've always wanted to say that, but I didn't. I just decided gut this time. The next bullet will be the head. Sarah, don't move. I will shoot to kill if you try anything."

Alex lunged across Dolan and opened the passenger door. Dolan felt a warm, numb feeling ooze across his midsection. Blood covered his hands now. He needed to apply pressure.

Then Alex pushed him hard, and he landed on the gravel lining the side of the highway. For a second, he thought he had been shot again, but it had only been the impact of hitting the asphalt. He saw Sarah watching him from the back seat window, her pale face askew with concern and fear.

Another shot rang out. Dolan felt it in the ribs.

His breathing became ragged.

Darkness fell as he went under.

Chapter 59

Amelia wore large sunglasses to cover her swollen eyes. She remembered how Sarah always called them Mickey Mouse glasses because they were the size of Mickey's ears.

Trees whipped by the Suburban's tinted windows. Caleb sat beside her, his head back, eyes closed. The FBI department psychologist sat across from them in a seat that swiveled one hundred and eighty degrees. She had it turned around to face them.

Amelia wanted to avoid Tracy's stare, so she looked out the window at the landscape. She was curious how all this would change Sarah.

Everyone will be changed in some way, she thought.

After the phone incident in the hotel room, Tracy handled her differently, like she was talking to a porcelain doll.

She felt Caleb's hand creep into hers. She tightened her grip to reassure him she was still with it.

"Before we get there, can we talk about something?" Tracy asked, her voice so soft it came out a whisper.

Amelia didn't respond right away. She was in no mood for conversation. She didn't want to talk about the mysterious phone incident, nor did she want to hear what Tracy was thinking. The woman's fake concern was unnerving, and Amelia found it an intrusion on their ordeal. They were on their way to pick up Sarah. What was there to talk about?

Tracy had gotten the call that Sarah was safe with Dolan and that they were on their way to meet the FBI. Amelia and Caleb were immediately whisked into the Chevy Suburban, taking them to rendezvous with their daughter. They were mere minutes from meeting with their daughter, which meant no more department psychologists. No more questions.

Amelia turned her head and looked at Tracy. "Go ahead. What else would there be to talk about?"

Tracy looked from Caleb's face to Amelia's and back to Caleb. "Vivian."

Hearing her daughter's name from someone else caused her to recoil with a flood of memories. Back in the day, she was shopping with Vivian. Then, not being able to find her, the police got involved. Security cameras in the mall were scanned. The FBI came in on the case when there were sightings of Vivian crossing state lines. An overwhelming feeling of sorrow, guilt and worry consumed her. She'd held baby Sarah in her arms and swore it would never happen to her.

Thirty-four days after she was kidnapped, Vivian was found on a dirt road twenty-two miles from the mall where she had been taken. She had been raped and murdered. The killer was never caught. There had never been a DNA match. No idle talk in prison somewhere. No confession from a guilty heart. Nothing. Just her Vivian dead and no killer to pay for taking her baby from her.

Tracy leaned back in her seat. "Does Sarah know about Vivian?"

"What's this got to do with anything?" Caleb asked. "We're about to pick Sarah up. This is a great day. We get our daughter back."

"Okay, you're right. I'm sorry. I just wanted to see if what Sarah writes was somehow connected."

"It isn't," Caleb said.

Amelia looked back out the window. She wanted Vivian to call again. She would have to ask Sarah if she knew anything about Vivian.

Vivian said on the phone she was with Sarah.

But Sarah wasn't dead, and Vivian was.

It didn't make any sense.

Chapter 60

Gert drove up a cracked, broken driveway surrounded by dry baked earth that hadn't seen farm equipment in years. Dust covered the BMW as he slammed on the brakes. He stopped at an angle in front of the steps that led to the broken front door. The abuse of an unrelenting summer sun had peeled the dirty white paint on the door. It sat askew, held to the frame by the bottom hinge.

Gert forced it back enough for him to enter the darkened interior but not enough to break it. He wanted to make it difficult for pursuers to enter.

The interior of the farmhouse was dark at first. As his eyes adjusted, he could make out old pieces of furniture. It looked like an antique shop that hadn't been dusted since the items were set out.

He heard the helicopter buzz by outside. The rotors were so loud it was all he could hear for a moment.

He entered a room that looked like it had been a kitchen at one time. Now it just had a pile of wood in the center with outlines of where the cupboards and counter used to cover the walls. Paint was chipped and peeled all over the room. Although there was no electricity, he could see well enough because the only window in the south wall allowed the sun access.

He realized his mistake in holing up in the farmhouse. Soon the cops would storm the place. There was no way he could make it on the run. There were too many cops to hide from. Languishing in prison would kill him. He couldn't do the time. He thought of himself as a control freak, and being an inmate was a surrender of control. The only one who ever controlled him was his brother.

He looked across the room and saw an archway that opened to another hall. Two entrances to the kitchen and a pile of debris about three feet high in the center of the room made it a great spot for an ambush.

Gert sat under the window, his back against the wall, and listened as the helicopter made another pass.

He pulled his gun out, along with the remaining ammunition, and waited, resolved to the end that was before him.

Chapter 61

Sam didn't want to be a hero, but he was the only one at the farmhouse, and the perp didn't know it. After radioing in his position, he was told to stand down. Backup was on the way. An FBI negotiator and the HRT were minutes away.

What the hell would they need a negotiator for? he thought. *Sarah's safe, and no one is talking this asshole out of the farmhouse.*

Sam had seen this kind of situation a hundred times, and almost every time, the perp died, usually by a self-inflicted shot after a few hours of fruitless negotiation. Some idiots choose death by cop, whereby they come out of the farmhouse shooting at officers who are waiting with an arsenal. Others sit it out until the FBI storm the building. In this case, Sam knew the police would be glad to return fire because this asshole steals little girls and kills cops.

This man was headed for trouble, and Sam would be his only chance. If he could get him in handcuffs in the next five minutes, he could live to pay for his crimes.

This was also personal for Sam because it marked the end of the task force. This criminal had done a lot of damage, caused a lot of pain, and now even Sam would not escape the consequences.

However, an arrest like this would win Sam some much-needed credibility.

He checked his watch as he approached the broken building from the rear. About three to four minutes was all he could hope for. He had gotten a pretty good look at the place when he passed it after watching the BMW pull in. A small copse of trees planted on the north side sheltered him as he ran up to the wall. At the back of the house, a shell of a window long since broken revealed an empty room. Sam began lifting himself into the room with both hands applying pressure on the sill.

His peripheral vision caught movement to his right. With one quick motion, he released the sill, dropped his body to the ground, and pulled his gun.

The possibilities were quite thin for those beside him near the back wall of an abandoned farmhouse. With no one around for miles, it had to be the perp, but his eyes told him differently.

Alex, Dolan's assistant, was standing behind Sarah, holding her by the back of the neck.

Sam kept his gun at the ready.

"What's this?" he whispered. Why was Alex here with Sarah? He thought they were with Dolan on their way to meet the FBI.

"This is a problem," Alex said. "You are a problem."

"I'm here to arrest her kidnapper. Why would you bring Sarah here? Are you fucking nuts? And why are you holding on to her that way?"

"Drop your gun, Sam. We all don't need another dead cop on our hands."

Alex moved sideways enough to expose a weapon he held pointed into the small of Sarah's back. Sam had no idea how Dolan's assistant was involved, but he did what he was told, bending slowly to place his gun in the foot-long grass. When his eyes met Sarah's, he was surprised to see cool confidence. He didn't see fear which made him wonder if she knew something neither one of them did.

"Okay, Sam, here's how it has to work. The FBI will be in the area within a minute or so. I need you to leave us alone, but we're running out of time, so I want you to run, not walk."

"I'm not leaving Sarah alone with you."

"Then you'll die where you stand while you foolishly try to be the good guy against all odds. Don't be stupid. Turn around and get going."

Alex moved the pistol away from Sarah and aimed it at Sam. Sarah smiled and nodded at him.

After a couple of seconds of silence, Sam stepped backward. He could not think of another way to handle this. He was not even supposed to be there.

He jumped at the sound of a gun being discharged.

Alex had fired at him but missed.

Sam turned and ran for cover.

The next bullet knocked him off his feet. Sarah screamed as he lost consciousness.

Chapter 62

ALEX TURNED AND PUSHED Sarah toward the open window.

"Climb in," he said as he reached down and picked up the cop's gun.

Sarah stumbled and then righted herself. "Why are you doing this?" she asked. "You don't have to. It could end right now."

"Just get in before I kill you here." Alex stood back and waited as Sarah sized up the window.

"Tell me, what happened to your hair? You're one ugly fucker." Alex shook the gun back and forth for emphasis as he looked her up and down.

Ignoring his question, Sarah folded her arms across her chest. "I asked you why."

He knew she was stalling for time. With the cavalry coming any second, she would have a better chance of getting out of this *outside* the building than inside.

"I can see threats aren't intimidating enough for you. You're willing to test me. I like that in an adversary. In a few words, here's what is about to happen. We're going through that window. Then we're going to find Gert, who will be killed with Sam's gun. If Gert returns fire, you'll be in front of me. If he misses, the cop's gun will be needed for you. I walk out of here, the hero. Or, scrap all that. I can shoot you in the face right here, right now."

Alex turned at the sound of a vehicle approaching. It was an old dull blue pickup truck loaded with hay. He looked back at Sarah.

"Everyone will see that I tried to save you," he said. "But Gert shot the cop while he was running away in the field and then shot you before I got the chance to get to him. Everyone who knows of my involvement is dead, and I take over the psychic fair where Dolan left off. Get it?"

"There's only one catch."

"What's that?"

"I'm not going to die today. You are."

Anger rose in him with such power he punched the wooden wall of the farmhouse.

"You've got some balls, kid. I should shoot you right now for that comment." He pointed. "You're going through that window. You've got one second to decide."

Wind buffeted his hair. It cooled his brow where a sweat broke out as he anticipated the FBI's arrival.

"I'll go in because I know all I've got to do is remember to not thump, rip and tear. It's better to be savage. At least that's what the note said."

Alex didn't ask what she was talking about. While she hopped up and through the window, he took one final glance at the road and saw FBI vehicles converging in a small dust cloud.

Just in time, he thought as he followed Sarah inside and landed on the broken wooden floor of what was once a bedroom.

He grabbed Sarah's arm and began looking for Gert.

They headed for the kitchen area of the farmhouse.

Chapter 63

The temporary command post was coming together fast as Agent Hanover organized and briefed the Hostage Rescue Team leader. His team was taking up positions around the perimeter of the farmhouse.

She was interrupted as her earpiece buzzed with the news that Sarah's parents were waiting one hundred yards back on the country road with the department psychologist. She told the driver to wait for her signal to approach the command post because they hadn't located Dolan and Sarah yet.

Her tactical team radioed in. There was no sign of Sam Johnson, but his vehicle was found parked twenty yards from the farmhouse behind a small thicket of bushes and trees. The stolen BMW SUV was visible in front of the farmhouse, and a silver Honda was parked in the rear, behind a weathered barn. License plates identified it as belonging to Alex Stuart.

"Fergus," Hanover turned to her partner, "find out who this Alex Stuart is. And get me, Dolan, on the phone. I need to know Sarah's safe before we enter the farmhouse."

Her HRT commander called in that all his men were in position. Barricaded by the front of a Crown Victoria, her negotiator bellowed on a bullhorn. She saw no movement at the farmhouse. The negotiator continued his plea for a dialogue and a peaceful end.

Hanover grabbed her cell phone as it vibrated on her waist.

"Speak."

"We've got a problem."

She recognized Angus Tran's voice. "Go ahead."

"Dolan was just picked up by a traveling businessman five miles from here. He's on the way to the hospital. It looks like he's been shot more than once."

She couldn't believe what she was hearing. "Where's Sarah?" she asked, her voice rising.

"Dolan has been in and out of consciousness, but he told the businessman who picked him up to call us and tell us that Sarah was taken by the guy who shot him. It was his assistant, Alex Stuart."

Hanover lowered her phone and looked at the farmhouse. That meant Sarah was a hostage again. If Alex Stuart's Honda was parked in the rear of the farmhouse, that also meant Sarah was in there with two men. Could they be working together?

The HRT was calling in her earpiece, looking for the go-ahead. The negotiator had tried, but there had been no response from anyone in the building.

Thoughts assailed her at a rapid pace. All that she read while debriefing on this case was coming together. A couple of guys kidnapping for hire. The girl always comes home, but no perps get arrested. The psychic can pinpoint victims but not the criminals. That's how Dolan knew where the victims were. It would seem likely he's involved.

But then, why was he shot?

How important was Alex Stuart? She had no choice but to treat him as a hostile person.

Fergus spoke to her through her earpiece. Sarah's parents were on the move.

She lifted her wrist to talk into the cuff. "I thought I ordered them held back for now."

"They stepped from the vehicle to stretch their legs. Caleb walked a little ways from the Suburban and then bolted across the grass. He wasn't seen until, well, he should be right behind you."

Special Agent Jill Hanover turned around and saw a panting Caleb Roberts walk past one of the Crown Vic's parked a stone's throw from her.

Her radio crackled as the HRT reported an emergency. She listened as one of the men said he had found Sam. He was alive but losing blood fast as he had been shot. An ambulance was needed immediately, or they would lose another cop.

This operation is falling apart, she thought.

She turned to greet Caleb while she ordered Fergus to get an ambulance here *yesterday*.

Shots rang out from inside the farmhouse behind her.

Chapter 64

ALEX HAD JUMPED THROUGH the window behind Sarah. They were in a small bedroom. It had to be at least a hundred degrees where she stood, but she couldn't stop shaking. She felt it was a delayed stress reaction. Or maybe her body was finally giving out after days of malnourishment and adrenaline rushes.

The man who stood beside her checking his gun was probably more dangerous than Gert, yet she felt no fear. She remembered him watching her at the fair, lurking around. She had felt something strange about him then, but it wasn't fear.

Am I getting cocky? she wondered with a small sense of bravado.

Mistakes could happen if she got overconfident. She would have to watch herself, stay alert and be proactive. Keep a clear mind and seize any opportunity to escape if one revealed itself.

Alex stopped fiddling with his weapon and grabbed her arm above the elbow. He pushed her silently toward the gaping doorway. With no measure of stealth, Alex pushed her through the open door and into the hall, where she stopped. He was using her to draw fire from Gert. She could not let that happen, but at the moment, she felt powerless to stop it.

She wrinkled her nose at the smell of mold and the thickness in the air caused by the afternoon sun.

Even though they inched along the hallway, the worn-out boards beneath their feet left a creaking telltale sign of their approach. She would have to think fast. She needed to figure out what door Gert was most likely behind so she could duck Alex's grasp.

She would only get one chance. That task felt impossible. How could she ever know something like that? He could be in the attic, the basement, or even the next room.

The hallway opened up on the left to a bright, spacious living room. Sun beat through the broken glass of what was once the living room window. One foot in front of her on the right was another opening. It probably led to the kitchen.

A breeze floated through the broken living room window, gently cooling her. She could hear someone outside announcing through a loudspeaker that they were looking for a peaceful solution.

Alex tightened his grip on her arm to the point where circulation was cut off.

The speaker outside commanded everyone in the farmhouse to come out of the building with their hands raised. Alex was running out of time.

He motioned for her to continue with a nudge. It hit her then that the kitchen would be ideal for an ambush. It was the heart of the building and accessible from two sides.

Alex pushed. As she crossed the kitchen's threshold, she threw herself forward, half stumbled, half dove, for the inside wall on the other side of the doorway, keeping low.

It all became a blur of noise as the blasts deafened her. She felt disoriented. To her right was a mound of broken wood. Studs and pieces of drywall piled three feet high.

Her sheer will to survive in a room with two men firing weapons, both of whom wanted her dead, got her moving. She speed-crawled to the pile and grabbed a two-by-four with a long nail protruding from the end.

She stayed on her knees until the guns quieted. Alex remained on his feet, bleeding from a wound in his lower belly. She saw Gert with his back against the wall under the kitchen window.

Her mind thought wildly that this wasn't something eighteen-year-olds were supposed to be a part of.

Gert had blood circling in two areas of his chest. He had a dazed look on his face as blood gurgled from the corners of his mouth. He sputtered and coughed. Something about this scene pleased Sarah. She caught herself smiling at the finality of it.

Sometimes, people like Gert need to die.

As Alex stepped closer to Gert, Sarah got to her feet and edged around the pile of debris. She got to an arm's length from Alex as he took the cop's gun and tossed it over his shoulder. He reached for Gert's gun.

She knew she should get out of this place. Here was her chance. But could she get out that window and around the corner before he was on her? Should she run or attack him?

She lifted the wood in her hands in defense, not sure what would happen. She didn't like this role. She wanted to help people. She realized in the same thought that she *was* helping. She was *saving herself.*

Alex was on his knees, fumbling with Gert's hand to get his gun. With the nail jutting out on the side of the wood in her hands, Sarah swung it at him.

But Alex was quicker.

He turned toward her, and a flash of lightning erupted from his hand as the nail embedded itself in his shoulder.

Sarah felt something punch her on the left side of the chest so hard she spun on her feet and fell to her knees. No pain accompanied the impact immediately. She could see the gun in Alex's hand.

It would look like Gert had killed her and shot Alex, too. The boss would walk out alive, and all evidence would die in the farmhouse.

Her mind raced back to what she had written.

... don't thump, rip and tear, better to be savage ...

She pulled the two-by-four hard to yank the nail out of his flesh. It must have hit the bone because it seemed stuck. Alex screamed and raised the gun again. She jerked and pulled, dislodging her weapon.

She had one last try.

She swung on a smaller arc. Before Alex could fire his weapon, the nail dug into Alex's neck below his ear, about where the jaw pivots. He screamed again and dropped the gun just as it had leveled with her head.

His hand found the business end of the wood and tried to pull it out. Before he could, Sarah turned her body away from him, holding the stud in an iron grip, and yanking the wood with her.

The nail pulled itself through the flesh of his cheek, ripping it wide open on a trail to his lips.

She fell to the floor with his screams piercing her consciousness. She saw blood everywhere, spilling over his hands as he struggled to keep it in.

Her chest was on fire now. Her breathing became shallow as pain echoed through her.

The scene became surreal as voices assailed her from all sides. She wondered if she had been too cocky after all.

She opened her eyes. It was such a struggle.

She saw men in shiny black helmets and suits carrying what looked like assault rifles.

Then she blacked out, minus the pen and paper.

Chapter 65

Sarah felt thirsty. Her mouth was so dry that it ached when she moved her tongue. Each attempt to swallow created a small stab of pain.

She kept her eyes shut as she listened.

Someone had to be told how thirsty she was. She felt her mouth hanging open. Maybe that's why it was as dry as dust. When she pressed her lips together, breathing became a little more difficult. Something was in her nose. Her body felt foreign to her as it rebelled with aches and pains.

She got her eyes open to small slits. Light came from a small lamp on a table beside the bed she lay in. It was almost too bright to keep her eyes open. She turned left to avoid its direct rays but stopped when a sharp pain shot through her shoulder.

When the pain subsided to a dull ache, Sarah was asleep again.

***

Sarah fought her way up by rising out of a storm, swimming deep, and searching for the surface.

She opened her eyes with a start. Her mouth was so dry it felt like she was massaging sand around her tongue. A nurse was just leaving the room. Sarah took in her surroundings.

She was in a hospital room, flowers filling a table by the window. The sun beamed in through the blinds. Her mother was asleep in a padded chair, a book in her lap.

"Mom," she moaned. "Mom?" she tried again.

Her mother turned her head and woke up. The paperback dropped to the ground as she jumped from her seat.

"You're awake," she stammered. "Oh baby, how do you feel?"

"Thirsty."

Her mother grabbed a bottle of water and straw beside the bed and carefully placed it on Sarah's lips. The pain was still there when she swallowed, but now she knew why. The two plastic tubes in her nose worked their way around and down the back of her throat.

"What are the ... tubes for?"

"The doctor said something about nourishment. They go to your stomach. You've been asleep for over two days. I'm so happy you're back."

Sarah sucked on the straw, then laid her head back. "Me too."

"We've got a lot to talk about. We met Mary Bennett. It seems you've been up to some kind of hero business. I don't know the whole story, but I'd like to hear your version."

Sarah nodded and looked down at the mound of bandages covering her gunshot wound.

"First, I'd like you to tell me about my dead sister."

***

The next couple of days were a blur. Constant visits from the FBI for statements, more flowers arriving daily. Denise, the woman from the construction trailer who got shot in the foot, came by to see how she was doing. Dolan came in a wheelchair. He was lucky as both bullets missed vital organs and didn't even nick a bone.

Sam Johnson never came to see her, but she heard he had survived his wounds.

Mary Bennett was one of the most emotional visits. Sarah was kidnapped and had to endure what she spared Mary from, yet Mary felt responsible. It didn't help that she covered for Sarah the night she was taken.

Esmerelda wouldn't stop hugging Sarah.

The most unusual visitor came at random times and spoke of societal decay. She also talked about the future and how it would be safer. Previous mistakes could be avoided.

This visitor spoke through Sarah's pen.

Her sister Vivian said when the time was right, she would tell Sarah who

had raped and killed her all those years ago.
    That man was still out there …

245

Chapter 66

Four years later …

Aaron Beck lowered his newspaper at the sound of the bus rounding the corner. He folded it under his arm and fished for the proper change in his pocket.

What did buses charge nowadays anyway? He hadn't ridden a bus since he was a teenager. With his car in the shop and his wife Carol working downtown today, he had no choice but to use the public transit system.

The bus pulled up, and the accordion-like doors slid open. Three passengers stepped on before him. He approached the driver, paid his due, and walked to the back, which was relatively empty.

He opened his paper and continued reading it. He was so absorbed in his perusal of the news he barely noticed the girl staring at him. His peripheral vision caught her after a few moments.

She was a young woman of about twenty-two, with blonde hair layered just past her shoulders. For her age, she was a stunner.

She had a pad of paper nestled in her right hand, with her left hand scribbling on it.

Then Aaron's eyes were caught in her stare.

Her intensity startled him. It was an unsettling feeling, causing him to peel his eyes away.

He tried to read his newspaper but couldn't focus. He lowered the paper and glanced outside.

Less than a second later, he was drawn into her fierce stare, unable to pull away.

There was no way he knew this girl.

He was about to ask her why she was staring when she signaled the driver that she wanted off the bus.

Then she walked over and dropped the notepad into Aaron's lap.

"You don't know me and have no reason to believe me. You've got less than six minutes to save your wife's life. She and three of her friends are about to cross Front Street downtown. The worker's truck is without a driver, and your wife won't make it." She glanced at her watch. "Call Carol now. There are only five-and-a-half minutes left."

The bus slowed to a stop, and the young girl headed for the door.

Aaron watched her leave, mouth agape. What was she talking about? This had to be a joke. The strange girl just told him that his wife was going to die.

He looked down at the notepad and quickly scanned what was written there.

"Hold it! I need off here, too," Aaron shouted.

Landing on the sidewalk, Aaron looked both ways.

The girl was nowhere in sight. He looked down at the pad in his hand again.

The words stunned him.

He pulled his cell phone out of his pocket.

Aaron could hear his wife's phone ringing on the other end. He wondered how much time remained.

Pick up. Don't tell me you left your cell phone in the office. Carol, please pick it up.

On the fifth ring, Aaron heard the music of his wife's voice.

She was still alive.

"Where're you?" he asked.

"Aaron, is everything all right?" Carol asked.

"Yes! Just tell me where you are."

"Okay, okay. I'm with a few of my girlfriends. We're walking downtown. We've decided to go for a coffee at this Danish pastry shop Marge is always talking about—"

"What street are you on?" Aaron asked. He could hear his voice cracking.

"Aaron? You sound—"

"*What street?*" he shouted.

"I don't know." Aaron heard her ask one of her companions what street they were walking on. "Dwight Street."

"Can you see Front Street ahead? Are you going to pass Front Street?"

"Yes, actually. I'm close enough now to read the sign. Why?"

"Stop! Don't go any farther." Aaron was sure he heard her footsteps halting.

"Aaron, tell me what's going on." Carol sounded agitated.

"This girl, on the bus." He was panting now, like he had run a race, his heart beating fast. "She wrote things on paper and told me you'd be dead in six minutes. I'm supposed to stop you from crossing Front Street."

"What girl? What's this about? I'm standing here with my friends. The sun is shining. It's a beautiful day. Everything's fine."

"I've never met this girl before, but she knows us. She wrote about my surgery when I was twelve and how you and I met. She jotted down your birthdate, middle name, and the year your parents died in that head-on collision when you were still a baby. Carol, no one could've known those things." Aaron grew hysterical as he continued to scan the area for any sign of the girl.

"What was that part about me dying?" she asked. "You aren't pulling my leg, are you? The lights ahead have changed to green. We're supposed to cross Front Street now."

"She told me to stop you from crossing Front Street. If you do, you'll die."

***

Carol's girlfriends had started without her.

She lowered the phone from her ear and looked from side to side.

That's when she noticed the dump truck.

Half a block up, road crews were repairing the asphalt.

It appeared no one had noticed the truck coming down Front Street. Through the windshield, the front seat looked empty.

There was no driver.

It was already gaining speed, barreling toward the crowd of pedestrians in the middle of the street.

Carol screamed for people to get out of the way.

Only six people of the twenty in the intersection heard her or chose to pay attention.

***

Sarah read the newspaper the next day. It reported two people were seriously injured, and seven were critical. None of the wounded were Carol or Carol's friends. They had held back just enough.

She would have to work harder if she was going to help people. Accidents like yesterday's might have been avoided if she had stuck around and talked to Carol on the phone herself. All those people were needlessly injured.

She also knew that she had to be ready.

She picked up her gun and made sure it was loaded.

Her sister's killer was still out there.

He didn't know she was meeting him in seven hours.

"I'm coming, asshole. I'm fucking coming."

About Jonas Saul

Jonas Saul is the bestselling author of the Sarah Roberts Series—more than two million sold!—and has written and published over sixty thrillers. After acquiring an agent, he signed several deals in Los Angeles, with MadRiver Pictures optioning his Sarah Roberts Series —over forty books!—(currently in development).

Jonas has often outranked Stephen King and Dean Koontz on Amazon over the past decade. He's regularly invited to be a guest speaker, teacher, or workshop presenter at international writing conferences and film festivals worldwide. He hosts an annual writer's retreat in Greece, where he currently lives. He focuses his teaching on how to get tension and emotion in every scene, on every page, how he made it as a creator/writer, the path to success in this business, and the pitfalls to avoid. He also hosts a reading retreat in Greece with guest authors, yoga retreats, and hiking retreats. Visit the Imagine Greece Retreats website at www.imaginegreeceretreats.com, or email him directly to discuss an opportunity to join one of the retreats at jonas@imaginegreeceretreats.com.

Jonas is also a professional freelance editor. He works for several publishers and does private editing for clients, with many testimonials on his website at www.imaginepress.org, which details each author's response to Jonas's editing skills. Email Jonas directly for an editing quote at editor@imaginepress.org.

To book Jonas for a speaking engagement at a writer's conference/festival, to have him on your jury at a film festival, or even to say hello, email Jonas directly at jonassaul@icloud.com.

For updates on releases, hit the "Follow" button on Amazon or Bookbub, and join Jonas on Facebook, where he's most active.

Contact Jonas Saul

Linktree: Find me here

Email: jonassaul@icloud.com

www.ingramcontent.com/pod-product-compliance
Lightning Source LLC
Chambersburg PA
CBHW060303310726
48976CB00007B/2198